Deep In The Heart

The McPhee Clan

Jillian Hart

Copyright © 2013 by Jill Strickler
All rights reserved.
http://jillianhart.net

Cover Design by Kim Killion, Hot Damn Designs
http://hotdamndesigns.com

E-book Formatted by Jessica Lewis, Authors' Life Saver
http://authorslifesaver.com

Editing by Jena O'Connor, Practical Proofing
http://practicalproofing.com

This is a work of fiction. Names, characters, places, brands, media, and incidents are either the product of the author's imagination or are used fictitiously. The author acknowledges the trademarked status and trademark owners of various products referenced in this work of fiction, which have been used without permission. The publication/use of these trademarks is not authorized, associated with, or sponsored by the trademark owners.

ISBN: 1494234122
ISBN-13: 978-1494234126

CHAPTER ONE

Montana Territory, November 1876

Annie McPhee gripped the stagecoach's door frame, deeply thankful the vehicle had stopped moving. Her head whirled and her stomach threatened to be sick, but since she'd skipped breakfast at the last stop, her stomach was thankfully empty. She let the chilly November air cool her sweaty face and climbed down the steps to the frozen-hard street.

"Ooh, it's a really big town!" Bea, just fourteen, bounced down the steps and landed with a two-footed thud, skirts swishing. "It's so much bigger than Landville. Look at all the stores."

"I see." Annie's gaze roamed the covered boardwalk in front of them, the shop windows bright with pretty things—dainty lady's bonnets, shining black shoes, colorful dresses. All were far too fine for her pocketbook, but they were a sight to behold. Besides, it didn't cost anything to look. "Go ahead, Bea, but stay where I can see you. I need to talk to the driver."

"Oh, I will. *Thank* you!" Delighted, Bea dashed away, worn and patched shoes pounding first the dirt street and then the plank boards. Her blond braids bounced as she went, her delight palpable.

"Will you and your little sister be all right?" the kindly driver asked, his gray mustache twitching with a grandfatherly smile. His black eyes twinkled with concern. "You oughtn't to be alone in a strange town,

Miss. Back when you boarded, you said you had someone meeting the stage."

"That was the plan." Annie wrapped her scarf more tightly around her neck. "But the stage is early. I'm sure he'll be along."

Okay, that might be a fib, because she wasn't *exactly* sure. All kinds of things happened in this world, and just because the teamster she'd hired had given his word that he'd be here to meet her and Bea at the stage it didn't mean he would. Good intentions were one thing, she'd learned in her twenty-one years of life, but life didn't work that way. She thought of the quiet, stoic man whom she'd only formally met when he'd given her an estimate. She'd noticed him around town many times, not that she'd actually spoken to him, but folks thought well of him when she'd asked about his reputation. And he'd been so nice to her when he'd given her a very reasonable bid, that she knew she could trust him to keep his word. He was a good, dependable man. He'd promised to haul her few possessions from the back of her friend's mother's shed in Wyoming and meet her here at the stage.

Well, she thought, gazing up and down the street. There was no sign of him. She sighed, not exactly disappointed because she'd learned long ago not to count on a man, even one as dependable seeming as Mr. Adam Butler. There were Indian raids, broken axles, illness, accidents and taking the wrong road—all things that would have kept him from meeting her. Unlike her former "husband," Adam didn't seem like the type to intentionally mislead anyone.

Which was probably why she'd hired him and trusted him with her possessions. She turned her attention to the stagecoach driver.

"I was hoping you could tell me an inexpensive place to spend the night, just in case." She glanced over her shoulder to where Bea stood, coltishly slim, her ragged and patched clothing making her look like a street urchin, out of place in front of all the finery in those shop windows. "I need a hotel or something that would be safe for my little sister and me."

"Well, you go just around the corner two blocks. There's a green house with white trim, it's the only one that color on the street. Mrs. Dowdy rents out her bedrooms on occasion. You tell her Pete sent you over and she'll take good care of you." He bobbed his head once in reassurance, his worn brown Stetson shading his face from the winter sun.

"Thank you." Feeling better, knowing she at least had a back-up plan, Annie fetched two satchels from the pile of luggage the armed guard had thrown down (there had been a worry about robbers and Indian raids on the road). She cast one look up and down the street studying horses and riders, but not one of them was the handsome, brawny, dark-haired teamster she was looking for.

"Annie?" Bea's shoes knelled on the boards, coming closer. "You've never seen anything so pretty. Do you have time to come see?"

"I have all the time in the world for you." Sweet, sweet sisterly love brimmed her heart. Oh, it was so good to see Bea smiling and dancing around again, those beautiful blue eyes glimmering. Bea had been so sad in the orphanage, quietly enduring hardship and loneliness. At least that was over now, Annie thought, but that separation from her sister was a wound that still ached. "Let's go take a look. If you had all the money in the world, what would you buy?"

It was an old game of theirs, one Bea jumped to with delight. She dashed back to the first shop, where a display of lady's bonnets ranged from the serious, somber black to an array of both bright and pastel colors.

"The red one." Bea gave a dramatic sigh. "It's the perfect color for a Christmas bonnet."

"Silly, it's not even Thanksgiving yet." Annie smiled, rolled her eyes, happy to see her sister looking happy.

"But Christmas is coming," Bea said, studying the bonnet dreamily. "Wouldn't it be perfect? That red bow and the silk poinsettia on the band? But I'd have to have a fabulous dress to go with it. Which hat would you pick?"

"I wouldn't pick any of them," she said sweetly. "I already have everything I want. I have you and a job promised to me by our aunt. Life doesn't get better than that."

"Some people's lives do," Bea reminded her with a wistful sigh, "because they can really buy these things. Annie, you have to play the game. Pick a hat."

"I'd take the brown one because it's the most sensible." She hardly looked at it. She had no need of pretty things—unless you counted Bea. She nodded toward the next shop over. "Sounds like you have your hat figured out. What about a dress?"

"Oh! I know just the one." Bea charged over to the next set of windows, excited by the pretty frocks and gowns. It never hurt to dream.

That was one thing Annie had stopped doing that sad day when she'd buried her baby girl, just three days old. Her heart hurt too much to bear. She'd lost the greatest dream of all, and so what was the point in wanting anything else? In dreaming even a tiny bit?

But to keep her little sister happy (and Bea really did deserve that), Annie sidled up to the shop windows and listened to Bea debate between the red gown or the Christmas green one. Annie nodded and agreed, as if cheerful, but inside her heart hurt and hurt. And that was her own fault. She'd reminded herself of her loss, hadn't she?

She gave a sigh, unhappy with herself for thinking of those sad things. She may not be able to dream, but Bea could. No matter what, Annie vowed, she would make sure at least a few of her little sister's dreams would come true. Bea was going to have a better life. A much better life.

* * *

Adam Butler leaned back on the wagon seat, thick leather reins in his gloved hands, squinting through the bright morning sunshine at the woman standing alongside her little sister on the boardwalk.

Annie McPhee. His chest ached at the sight of her. Oh, it was good to see her. He'd missed her since the morning he'd driven away from the sorry excuse of a shed she had her things stored in on that Landville farm. He drew in a slow breath, because with the way he loved her, there simply wasn't enough room in his chest for air too.

She looked good. Better than before, he thought. He'd seen her laugh. The faint bell of her laughter reached him as he guided the horses around the stopped stagecoach, not taking his eyes from her. Gold curls cascaded over her slender shoulders. Her worn and patched brown coat draped her willowy figure. Her profile was adorable with a graceful fall of bangs, a sweet sloping nose, a rosebud mouth and a dear, dainty chin. He'd admired her from afar for so long, he hurt with a longing fierce enough to break steel.

This was his last chance, he knew, to try and win her heart. She had a job in a town not far from here and she would be living with family after being on her own for so long. There was no way she would ever go back to Landville and so if he didn't find a way to make her love him before he left her here, then she would be lost to him forever. He had to give this all he had.

Determined, he pulled the horses to a stop, the wagon gave a final jolt and rattle. He braced one elbow on his knee, watching as Annie shook her head.

"No, I'd never feel comfortable in such a bright red dress," she chuckled again, a happy sound, one he hadn't heard from her in so long. "I'd feel like a giant tomato walking around."

"A tomato?" little Bea asked, wrinkling up her nose. "Why a tomato?"

"It was the only thing I could think of that was bright red." Annie shook her head, scattering those blond curls. Her cheeks were flushed pink with her happiness and the bite of the icy late-November wind. "Maybe a big apple? Or a beet? Anyway, I'd feel much better with that brown dress."

"Brown?" Bea sighed dramatically. "This is supposed to be a fancy Christmas dress, you know, for a Christmas party. Nobody wears a brown dress to that."

"A dour old spinster might." Annie's voice caught, sounding false now, as if she were forcing that lightness into her words.

And he knew why. He hung his head, set the brake, understanding the toll her losses and hardships had taken on her. He climbed down, his boots hitting solid ground. He'd been the one to have the casket made for her daughter, although she hadn't known it. He'd paid for the burial, although she would never know that either. Reverend Brown and the carpenter back in Landville had promised to take that information with them to their graves.

That's what true love was, Adam knew, as he walked around the back of his wagon, leaving his team of horses to stand obediently alongside the street. Love was a verb, a selfless verb—doing for those you love without a thought for yourself. Even if she would never know all that he'd done for her.

"Ladies," he called out, tipping his hat as he stepped onto the boardwalk behind them.

"Mr. Butler!" Bea's delight was instant. Big smile, beaming eyes, a little happy hop. "I knew you'd come, I knew it. Do you still have our stuff?"

"Packed and covered tight, safe and sound in my wagon." He

pointed behind him where the waterproof tarp covered the meager pile of possessions. Extra clothes, a few crates of quilts and handmade items. A few pieces of old, battered furniture, all of sentimental value to Annie, which made them priceless. His gaze riveted to Annie, who'd turned to him and smiled with relief, her brown hat shading her face.

"Adam, it's good to see you here." Her gaze met his gratefully. Not the way a lady who was very glad to see him might look at him. No, there was nothing personal or special in the way she cast her light blue gaze to him. "The stage arrived early, and I see so did you."

"Yes." He'd been here for two days, hurrying through the long journey because he wanted to be sure he was here on time. For her. But he didn't know how to tell her that, so he stood there, a lump rising up to wedge solidly behind his Adam's apple. He suddenly felt too tall, too big and too rough for a dainty beauty like her. Words seemed to evaporate, but he cleared his throat and pushed past this shyness. "How was the ride?"

"Bumpy." Annie shrugged, her soft mouth curving upward with good humor.

"Yeah." Eager to agree, Bea tossed her twin blond braids over her shoulders. "Really, really bumpy."

"And that might not be over yet," he told them, "depending on the roads ahead. I've never been to Bluebell before, so we'll have to find out together."

"It really is nice of you to drive us." Annie's gentle, alto voice rolled over him, as sweet as a touch. Her eyes fastened on his, full of appreciation.

Appreciation, not fondness. Not liking. Not love. Well, that didn't stop him from wishing. Squaring his shoulders, he thought of the future. He'd stay in Bluebell until she was all settled in with her aunt. It wouldn't give him much time to make her see him differently, but it was a chance. That was something. Annie McPhee was the best, most lovely lady he'd ever set eyes on. For him it had been love at first sight, and that had been four long and lonely years ago.

"It's my pleasure to help out," he told her as offhandedly as he could, as if she was just another customer hiring him to haul her things. "Are you ladies ready to go?"

"Yes!" Bea gave a skipping sort of a hop, little-sister cute. She looked happy to be out of that orphanage.

"Then I'll just grab these." He swooped up the satchels on the boardwalk next to Annie, breathing in the faint scent of vanilla. His skin prickled being this close to her, and everything about her made a band cinch up tight about his chest—the rustle of her petticoats, the swirl of her skirt ruffle, the light, deliberate pad of her shoes on the board planks beside him.

He'd driven through bitter cold days, slept in his wagon shivering half the night, just to do this for her—bring her things here and drive her to Bluebell, just to be this close to her. It was worth it.

"Thank you, Adam." She smiled at him, following him into the street. The bright sun faltered as a cloud sailed in front of it.

"Don't mention it. I'm a teamster. Hauling things is what I do." He shrugged his wide shoulders and set the satchels in the back of the wagon. "I have some blankets folded on the floor for you ladies. It's going to be a cold ride."

"We don't mind!" Bea had already bounced up onto the wagon seat, claiming the middle spot. "Oh, I see another dress shop, Annie."

"No, we're not going to take the time to look at that one." Good-natured, Annie rolled her eyes. How she loved Bea's enthusiasm. She grabbed the wagon frame, ready to hop up onto the cushioned seat, but an iron-strong hand wrapped around her elbow, his heat scorching through her layers of clothing, burning her skin.

Very strange. Her pulse skipped a beat, stalling in her veins. She blinked up at him, surprised by her reaction to him. *I must be much colder than I realize,* she thought, as the wind gusted cruelly. First thing she'd do was to shake out those blankets and snuggle into them.

She placed her foot on the running board and stepped up, aware of Adam's heat and strength as he helped her onto the seat, the gentleman that he was, and let go. He tipped his hat, stepping back and she felt oddly aware of his presence in those few seconds before he backed away.

"Here, cover yourself up good," Bea instructed, already shaking out one of the blankets. "I gave you the warmest one."

"Maybe it would be better to share the blankets, so we warm each other," Annie suggested, hearing the faint fall of Adam's measured, powerful gait circling around the back of the wagon. A wagon passed by, rigging jangling, horse hooves clomping. Behind them the stage driver shouted out, "All aboard!" and that created all kinds of noise and clatter, but still it was Adam she heard as he climbed up on the other side of Bea. Very strange. Perhaps her brains had rattled around too much on that bumpy ride through Montana Territory, she thought, tucking the blanket in snugly.

"What about you?" she asked Adam, holding up the second blanket. "You'll need to stay warm too."

"Oh, I'm used to the cold." He wrapped his large hands around the thick leather straps, holding them like the expert horseman he was. "You and Bea use both of those blankets. And hold on, the boys are ready to go. They don't like standing in these temperatures."

"No kidding," Annie said as the four big chestnut bay horses lunged forward and merged into traffic. She caught sight of a few fancy buggies, but most folks drove wooden wagons. Snow clouds hovered in the north, a gray-white mantle slowly spreading across the crystal blue sky.

The town passed in a blur and suddenly they were turning down a road that took them away from buildings and homes and into wild meadows, where the wind whipped with haunted eerie notes and the shadows fell long. Desolate, she shivered beneath the blankets, wondering what lay ahead for her and Bea. What was Aunt Aumaleigh like? She reached into her pocket and pulled out the note, studying it quietly as Bea leaned forward, taking interest in a horse she saw in the field.

A wild horse, Adam informed her.

Annie bowed her head and began to read.

Dear Annie,

My name is Aumaleigh McPhee. I am your aunt. Your grandmother passed away last summer and I found your letter to her when I was going through some of her things. I am so sorry to hear of the hardship you were going through and while I hope it is resolved now and that you are all right, here is some traveling money if it is not. It is enough for stage passage to Deer Springs, the nearest stage stop to our little town of Bluebell. You should have enough left over to hire a horse at the local livery, or you can always send a message and I'll come to fetch you. I look forward to hearing from you, and if you do decide to come, please know you will be very welcome here. This is a big ranch and we can always find room for family.

DEEP IN THE HEART

With love,
Aumaleigh

Very grateful that money had bought not just one first-class ticket as her aunt had intended, but two lower class tickets, Annie folded up the note. She slipped it back into her pocket, daring to hope. Just daring. Hoping wasn't dreaming, she thought. It was practical, it was sensible, wanting a job and a place to stay. It wasn't as if she wanted more.

Troubled, she blew out a sigh, remembering that time more than a year and a half ago now when she'd lost her job and been so desolate and in need. Homeless, penniless, without any way to pay for her baby's casket. If the town carpenter hadn't donated it, saying he'd never charged for babies, she didn't know what she would have done. She'd written to her grandmother but had never received an answer until Aunt Aumaleigh's recent letter.

Please let this be a good thing, she thought, wishing it with her whole heart. For the past few years, life had been one hardship after another and there was a point when a person couldn't take anymore, not without losing what remained of her heart. All she needed was a job and the chance to turn her luck around, for Bea's sake.

She slipped her arm around the girl. Bea happily scooted over, snuggling in, just the way they used to do when they were much younger. Adam was right—the ride was a cold one, with the wind icy enough to numb her face and make her eyes sting, but she and Bea were together.

Grateful, she glanced over the top of her sister's head at the man behind the reins. It was too cold to talk, Adam had drawn his scarf up over his face, so that only his dark blue eyes showed. He was a well-built, muscular man, over six feet tall, but he was a gentleman. His face was sculpted granite, with high, chiseled cheekbones, a straight blade of a nose, and a strong, stubbled jaw. He was handsome. Very handsome. Why hadn't she ever noticed that before?

Maybe because she was through with men. Her heart was so broken and disillusioned there was no way she was going to love again. She'd stopped believing it was possible for her. Besides, she didn't want it to be. A place to live, a good job and taking care of Bea. These were her hopes for her life—the only ones that mattered.

CHAPTER TWO

It was a frigid ride, just over an hour, rolling through meadows and hills, heading straight for the snow-covered mountains. Annie cast a sidelong glance at Adam, sitting powerfully still and strong on his side of the seat, holding the reins in his gloved hands. To look at him, you wouldn't know he was freezing, but he had to be. Then again, she reasoned, he was a teamster. He probably drove like this all winter long.

"Oh!" Bea scooted forward on the cushion, allowing a stream of wind to slide beneath the blankets, and yanked her scarf from her mouth. "I think I see the town. Is that it, Mr. Butler?"

"Looks like it to me." Adam's deep baritone rumbled kindly, but then he fell back into silence. Which was fine with her, as it really was too cold to talk.

She gestured for Bea to sit back and went to the task of tucking the blankets firmly around them, doing her best to keep her teeth from chattering. Fresh snow mantled the tall, spellbindingly beautiful mountain, and the wind carried the scent of that snow. Overhead, the sky had gone completely white-gray, thick with the promise of a coming storm.

"Annie? We're almost there." Bea bumped Annie's arm with her own, practically vibrating with excitement. "What do you think our room will be like? What do you think Aunt Aumaleigh will be like? Do you think she'll like me?"

"Of course, she will. She'll love you. Who wouldn't like you?" She nudged Bea right back, smiling with her eyes because her scarf was covering her mouth.

"Right, I forgot how popular I am," Bea joked, rolling her eyes adorably. Oh, and she was so adorable with her big soulful blue eyes, her button nose and her dear personality. The sadness from the orphanage still lurked in the shadows of her eyes, however, as she gazed at the town that was growing closer, more than just a smudge in the hollow of a vast mountain valley, the sadness seemed less than it had been yesterday.

"Oh, that's our new town," Bea breathed, studying the distant buildings. Gray smoke puffed up from chimneys, giving it a cozy look.

"Yes it is. It's our new start, just you and me." Annie slipped an arm around her sister's shoulder and drew her in to give her a sisterly snuggle. Surely at the back of Bea's mind she was worrying that this might not work out. Well, that was Annie's worry deep down too. But the warm and loving words from their aunt's letter came back to her, chasing away that doubt. No, she had to stay positive. She had to believe their luck was about to change.

"Do you ladies have directions to the ranch?" Adam pulled down his scarf and broke the silence, asking his question with his gaze straight ahead on the bumpy road. The four horses, in matching shades of chestnut, dutifully clomped through mud and standing water, their gaits in unison.

They were just like their owner, she thought. Dutiful, to the point, got the job done, didn't have much to say.

"Sorry, our aunt didn't send any directions." She pulled down her scarf and offered him an apologetic smile. "I guess I hadn't thought that far ahead. I could ask someone when we get to town."

"That's my job, to deliver you safely there." A small smile hooked the corner of his chiseled mouth. He said nothing more, falling back into silence again, but there was a solid, dependable quality to him that remained like warmth in the air. It made her glad she'd chosen him to haul her things. It had concerned her mostly because of the low bid he'd given her. An extremely low bid.

He must need the money, she thought, knowing just how that felt. Without the hundred dollars Aunt Aumaleigh had sent in her letter, Annie would still be struggling at her old jobs cleaning at both the hotel and the saloon. Bea would still be at the children's home. She hoped one day good things would come Adam's way too.

"Look! It's the town!" Bea bounced up again, eager for that first look down the main street, frozen in some places, muddy in others. "Oh, it's tiny! Why, I can see from one end to the other."

Tiny was right. Annie counted eight blocks in all, with a livery barn and a lumberyard across from it, marking the far end of the street. The buildings rose two stories high with a few trees at the corners of the cross streets to add a bit of shade come summer. Only a few folks were out and about, clipping speedily down the boardwalks, perhaps on last minute errands before the storm hit. A donkey and cart was parked at a hitching post halfway down the street.

Adam drew his double team to a stop near the cart and pulled the brake. The sign swinging in the wind, squeaking slightly on rusty hinges, proclaimed *Gunderson's Mercantile* in bright blue letters. The feed store across the street had a handwritten sign in the window that said *closed for lunch, be back when I'm done.*

Interesting. This was an even smaller place than Landville and that was really saying something.

"I don't see anywhere to eat," Bea leaned in to whisper to her. "I'm really hungry."

"Me, too," she whispered back, watching as Adam laid the reins on the dashboard. He rose out of the seat, climbing down.

"I'll get directions," he said succinctly, a muscle in his strong jaw working. He took a deep breath. "Want to come in and warm up for a minute?"

"I can't say no to that." Annie smiled at him across the top of Bea's head. That was nice of him to give them a break from the cold weather, especially since he was paid by the job and not by the hour. His time was money, and yet he didn't make her feel rushed.

"Let's get you down first, Miss Bea." He held out his hand to the girl, stoically helping her to the ground. When he held out his hand again, he seemed to be blushing slightly. Likely it was from the bite of the cold wind. "Miss Annie."

"Thank you." She laid her gloved hand on his leather-gloved palm. Again, her pulse hitched but this time she understood her reaction to his good manners. It was Harold, she realized. Harold's courtesy toward her had ended the moment the minister had pronounced them man and wife. All the doors that slammed in her face, all the wagons she had to climb down from when she was pregnant haunted her now, pulling up the sadness she didn't want to remember.

But it did feel good to have Adam's common courtesy, to feel as if she were as valuable as any other woman. She pushed off the seat and climbed to the ground, thankful to him as he nudged her forward at the last minute, so her skirts wouldn't drag in a muddy puddle.

Yes, she really did appreciate Adam's gentlemanly ways.

"What do you think of the town?" he asked her in his rumbling, deep voice, so pleasant that it reminded her of a slow, masculine song.

"It has a friendly feel to it," she decided as she climbed the handful of steps from the street to the boardwalk. "It feels like the promise of good things to come."

"I hope it will be." He dipped his chin for emphasis, his dark blue eyes warm. He towered next to her on the boardwalk and reached to haul open the heavy door. A bell tinkled overhead. "After you, ladies."

"Ooh, it feels so warm!" Bea traipsed in, shoes tapping, braids bouncing. "And it smells so good. Hey, Annie. They have candy."

"You can look, but don't touch," she reminded her little sister. Eager footsteps drummed against the store's floorboards as Bea headed straight for the glass canisters full of colorful candy at the far end of the front counter.

"Welcome," greeted a woman who stood behind the counter. Her black hair was drawn sleekly up into a fashionable up knot of curls and swirls. She wore a lovely but sensible brown dress. She arched a slender brow at Adam. "You look new to town. How can I help you?"

"Howdy, ma'am. I'm in need of directions, please." Adam hiked closer, staring down at the boards in front of his feet as if shy. He made quite a picture standing there, so big and straight and tall with his muscular strength at rest. The lamplight shone almost blue in his black hair, catching on the black whiskers stubbling his iron jaw. "The ladies are looking for a ranch. Their aunt's ranch."

"There's only one lady who owns a ranch in these parts." The woman softened, her friendly look becoming even more kind as she cast her gaze in Annie's direction. "You must mean Aumaleigh. I had no idea there were more McPhee girls. I'm Gemma. It is so good to meet you."

"I'm Annie. It's nice to meet you, too." She approached the counter without realizing she'd even taken a step. Nothing felt better than being greeted by such open, genuine warmth. She felt as if she'd already made a friend. Her worries felt less heavy as she smiled at Gemma. "That's Bea over there. It sounds as if you know our aunt."

"Very well. To know her is to love her. You'll see." Gemma's eyes shone with certainty, and grateful tears smarted behind Annie's eyes.

"You'll want to go back through town," Gemma explained to Adam, all business. "Follow the fork in the road left, going right will take you straight back to Deer Springs. You just stay on that road until you see the entry gates to the Rocking M Ranch, about a mile or so out of town. You can't miss it."

"That sounds easy enough." Adam tipped his hat, his gaze still on the floor. "Much obliged, ma'am."

"My pleasure," the shop clerk answered pleasantly. "Is there anything else I can help you with?"

He hesitated, not quite able to take his attention from Annie. She'd moved over to the pot-bellied stove, peeling off her gloves to warm her hands. She stood a little straighter, seemed a little brighter. He felt sincerely glad, all the way down to the bottom of his heart, to hear this aunt of Annie's was kindly. Annie deserved that, she really did.

"You wouldn't happen to have a can of axle grease?" he asked, knowing he'd used the last of his supply when he'd stopped for the night down in Dillon. He didn't need it now, but it gave him an excuse to purchase something, so he could buy a stick of candy for Annie's little sister without Annie realizing it—until it was too late. One look at Annie told him she wished she had the penny to spare. He had no problem sparing one of his for her.

"The axle grease is three aisles over, right in the middle of the shelf, eye-level," the shop clerk answered cordially. "I can fetch it for you."

"No, don't bother. I can find it." He was used to doing things for himself and besides, it would give the ladies a chance to visit. Annie was going to live in this town, and she needed friends. It had been hard for her to leave her friend behind in Wyoming.

He stole a peek at her as he strolled down the aisle, watching as she unbuttoned her coat, warming up in the stove's heat. Basking there, she couldn't have been prettier with her delicate, heart-shaped face, pink from the cold weather, her blue eyes bright with hope. Catching him looking at her, she threw him a small smile, just a tweak of the corners of her soft, Cupid's bow mouth. It was an appreciative smile, one that made his heart surge with hope. He was thinking that she was starting to notice all he did for her and maybe the kind of care he was capable of giving her.

That hope felt good. Very good. Adam circled into the third aisle, searching the shelves for the can of grease. Once Annie and her little sister were thawed out, he would take them the last mile of their journey. Annie would need to get settled in, he figured. If the aunt didn't have a place for her to stay, then he'd help her with that. And if the aunt had a spare room, then she would need help moving the furniture. Likely she would let him help with that, he thought, spying the can he was searching for and snaring it off the shelf. The hope in his heart grew stronger as he headed down the aisle, circling back to her. He'd be here to help her as much as he could.

"Good morning, my fair lady," a man's voice rose from the front of the store, rumbling over the ring of the bell from above the front door. "Are you new to our quaint little town, or just passing through?"

"Oh, I'm new here," Annie answered, her dulcet, gentle alto warm and cordial. "I have a job waiting for me on my aunt's ranch."

"Aunt's, hmm?" The man's tenor rumbled full of confidence. "You must mean Aumaleigh McPhee. She's my neighbor."

"Wonderful," Annie said politely. It was a sword to Adam's gut that it sounded as if she meant it.

He skidded to an abrupt halt at the end of the rows of shelving, seeing her and the newcomer together for the first time. She'd peeled off her gloves, untied her hat and couldn't have looked prettier as she beamed a polite smile at the man. A man who was average height, a little on the slim side, with a handlebar mustache and shoulders that said he didn't do hard physical labor to make a living. He appeared bookish, just like Harold Marcus had been. If Annie had a type of man she preferred, then he was it.

Adam felt his hopes deflate. Especially with the way this new man had puffed up his chest, swept off his bowler hat and grabbed Annie's slender hand up in his to kiss her knuckles.

"Lawrence Latimer, at your service, lovely lady." He grandly released her hand and bowed like he was in the queen's court. "How can I help you? I saw your wagon outside. I could ride along with you and help you unload it."

"Uh—" Taken aback, Annie blushed, and before she could accept this interloper's help, Adam strode out, boots knelling on the wood floor, jealousy and anger welling up like hot lava from a latent volcano.

"That's my wagon." He let his voice boom territorially, letting this dandy (who was much shorter than he was, by the way) know beyond all doubt that he was trespassing. Annie McPhee was already claimed—although she didn't know it yet. At least, he still had that hope. Until she turned him away and he drove out of this town, he had hope—and he was going to cling to it. He fisted his hands, fighting to keep his emotions out of his voice. "I'll see to the lady."

"Sorry, sir, I didn't know the lady was with anyone." Lawrence Latimer visibly gulped and went pale. He plopped his hat back onto his slightly bald head. "My profound apologies to you too, Miss."

"Oh, Adam is a teamster," Annie corrected in her quiet way. Her words made the sword in his gut slip deeper. She looked down, looking uncomfortable. "Adam has been kind enough to haul our things, for my sister and me."

"I see." That twinkle leaped back into Latimer's small brown eyes. He took a step forward. "Perhaps there's some way I can assist? Perhaps help you save some of the fee for unloading the wagon?"

"No," Adam thundered, surprised by the hard, angry echo of his voice resounding on the mercantile walls. Everyone stared at him in shock, including the shop clerk. Bea walked away from the candy display, her gamine face pinched up with worry.

"I mean," Adam explained, clearing his throat, needing to fix the damage. Any moment Annie was going to put two and two together and figure out how he felt for her—before he could show her he was a man she could trust. He felt his face heat and he charged forward to thunk the can of grease on the counter. "I'm not charging an unloading fee. I know Annie. We're friends."

"Oh." Latimer looked sly as he seemed to consider that.

Great, Adam thought, pulling out his billfold. Now, he'd made himself sound like he'd been friends with her for years—*friend* being the operative word. He gritted his teeth, ready to curse himself for that stupid move, but then he hadn't given it any forethought. He'd been too busy being mad and jealous. Not a good combination, and not one he'd ever felt before. As strong as he was, he was helpless to stop it.

"Then perhaps I'll pay a visit later on," Latimer proposed as he tipped his hat to Annie one more time, offering her what he supposed passed for a debonair grin. "To check and see how you're settling in."

"Well, I—" Annie shook her head, looking ready to say no.

"It's the neighborly thing to do, especially in these parts," Latimer wisely interrupted her, talking over his shoulder, prancing down the long aisle between the tall rows of shelves. "I'll look forward to the pleasure, my lady."

My lady? Adam fumed as he tossed a greenback on the counter. Yeah, he wanted to punch that guy. Instead he fought down his temper and caught the storekeeper studying him. Understanding flashed in her eyes and she nodded her head once, smiling sadly at him as if she'd guessed the truth.

Maybe it was a lost cause, he thought miserably as he gestured toward the candy display. For the better part of the last two years he'd been trying to get up the nerve to ask to court her. And for the better part of that time, Annie had shied away from him, walking with her head down, not making eye contact. He'd been at a loss. That would not happen this time. He lowered his voice to a whisper to the clerk. "And please add two sticks of whatever candy the little girl seemed to like."

"Of course." The clerk moved away, lifting the lid off one of the glass canisters, but his heart was too heavy to notice much else as he turned to study Annie still standing at the stove, washed in lamplight.

"Everyone seems to have a nice tone in their voices when they mention Aumaleigh," she was saying in a low voice to her little sister. "It bodes well, don't you think?"

"Oh, yes." Bea gave a little hopeful nod. "Maybe everything is going to be okay now. Maybe we'll have family, someone to help you, Annie."

Family, Adam thought with both despair and gratefulness as he accepted his change from the clerk. He pocketed the money. If Annie's family accepted her warmly, stepping up the way family was supposed to do, then that would be a great improvement in her life. She'd been struggling for so long all by herself, shooing away any man who came courting or who even looked her way—and with good reason. Her reputation had been ruined beyond repair in Landville. She deserved this fresh start with good people who cared about her.

And as much as he wanted that for her, it meant his chances with her were much less. If she had family, then she wouldn't need his help for much longer. She didn't need him. What if she shooed him away like all the rest of the men who came her way over the years?

His chest went tight at the thought, his heart felt hollow. The shop clerk finished wrapping the grease can for him and had tucked both candy sticks into a little white paper bag. She gave him a sympathetic look as she handed over his purchases.

"Thank you," he told her, not sure if he meant for the candy or the sympathy. He was a sorry case, he thought to himself as he crossed the floor, longing for a woman who'd never looked at him twice. Maybe that meant the only consolation was that she wouldn't look at that Latimer fellow twice either.

"Oh, did you get some candy?" Bea's eyes went wide, spotting the paper bag he carried. "Which kind did you get? They're all so pretty, I couldn't pick if I tried."

"I don't know, the shop lady chose for me." He held out the bag to the girl, but his gaze arrowed to Annie who was buttoning up her coat, having noticed he was ready to go. It was true that she didn't look at him with love sparkling in her dazzling light blue eyes, but for a moment he pretended she did. Tenderness ebbed into the hollow places in his chest, into the lonely places in his heart. "I thought you two ladies would like something sweet to celebrate the day. You're almost home."

"Really?" Breathless, disbelieving, Bea hesitated, shaking her head, as if she was sure she'd misheard.

But Annie's eyes filled with tears. Silvery and sweet and full of gratitude.

Gratitude. That got to him, and a lump rose in his throat.

"Adam." She tugged on her gloves, her gaze lingering on his. For a moment, his heart leaped and it was as if he could feel her heart in that gaze, that singular, momentary connection. Then she smiled. "That was very thoughtful of you."

"It's my pleasure." He meant every word. Afraid he'd revealed too much, he bowed his head, breaking the moment between them.

"Thank you, Mr. Butler." Bea's hand shook as she finally took the bag he'd been holding out. "Thank you so very much."

"You're welcome, kid." He opened the door, clearing his throat as the bell overhead chimed away. He let the cold air blast his face, felt the brush of a snowflake against his cheek. When he looked back, Annie was watching him, hand on her sister's shoulder as she steered the girl toward the doorway. Bea clutched the candy bag carefully, as if it were too precious to actually open.

"Thank you, Adam," Annie said, on her way out the door. It felt as if she saw him differently as she swished away.

CHAPTER THREE

"Annie?" Bea broke the silence that had settled in as they jostled along the country road. "Where do you think we're gonna end up living?"

"I don't know, probably someplace on the ranch, I guess." She patted her reticule, thinking of the money inside, precious little funds she'd squirreled away over time as well as some of the tiny bit of change leftover from the stage fare. "I guess we'll see when we get there."

"But we'll be together," Bea said thinly, as if she needed to be reassured one more time.

"Of course, silly. I'm not going to barter you away for a house or something. I'm going to keep you around." She lightly elbowed Bea in the side. "Then again, maybe I'd rather have a house."

"Maybe we can get one someday." Bea brightened at that. "I saw some streets full of houses as we drove out of town. Do you think we could get a house of our own?"

"I don't think I'll make enough for that, at least not right away." She hated to disappoint her sister, but in her experience people tended to pay menial workers (which she was) as cheaply as they could. She couldn't expect her aunt to pay her more than her work was worth. Maybe it would have been different if she'd been able to finish school. She could be making a schoolteacher's wages, enough to afford a small place for her and Bea. As it was, they could not be choosey. "We'll be grateful for what we get. As long as the roof is good and the walls sturdy, that is good enough for me."

"Yeah, I know. That's true," Bea agreed with a determined nod, scrunching her face up for a moment with the effort to keep from hoping for too much.

Annie knew just how that felt. Nerves flitted around in her stomach and dampened her palms. She slipped a gloved hand out from beneath the warm blankets to rub a snowflake from her eyelash. Tiny flakes swirled tenaciously to the ground so the road stretching ahead of them was flocked white.

"I could find out what houses rent for in Bluebell," Adam offered from the far side of the wagon seat. Staring straight ahead, his eyes on the road, he cleared his throat and gave a casual shrug. "If you wanted, that is. A shanty might be reasonable way out here. Property prices are a lot less here than in Landville."

She hadn't thought of that. She gazed around, tipping her head back to look up at the jagged, mysterious mountains rimming the snowy valley, their peaks lost from sight in the shroud of white-gray storm clouds. It seemed isolated at this far edge of the territory, so maybe there was hope for affording a shanty one day. She saw nothing but land in every direction. Herds of cattle huddled in fields, tree-mantled hillsides and the wink of a river in the distance, but that was all.

What if they could have their own place, just her and Bea? It didn't have to be fancy, just warm and solid. And maybe it could be close enough so Bea could walk to school. More hope built inside her and Annie smiled. This was a new start for them. Please, let it be a good one, she thought. *Please.*

"Looks like we're here." Adam lifted a hand toward the sign dangling between two tall posts. "The Rocking M Ranch."

"Yes, I guess this is the moment of truth." Annie huddled beneath the blankets, taking it all in—the expanse of land, pasture and mountains in the background. Neat wooden fencing lined a lane on either side, giving way to sloping fields swathed with fresh snow. A few horses looked up, their manes snowy, gazes curious as Adam reined his team off the country road.

"Are you nervous?" Adam asked. "Because you look it."

"Yes. Absolutely." She blinked against the wind driving snow into her face, feeling the flicker of nerves turn into a serious flutter. "I've never met anyone from this side of the family before. It's been so long since Bea and I have had real family, I'm not sure if my hopes are too high or too low."

"It will be fine. You have nothing to worry about," Adam said as the horses diligently climbed the slope, heads bowed to the task. The regard and reassurance in his tone made her feel as if they weren't such strangers after all. He'd been thoughtful enough to buy Bea candy, a luxury she hadn't had in far too long (Bea still hadn't opened the bag yet).

Annie smiled at him with her eyes, since her face was covered by her scarf. "There was a rift in the family. Our father was disowned long before I was born."

"Are you afraid they might not accept you?" he asked, arching a dark eyebrow.

"No. I'm afraid I might be a disappointment to them," she confessed as the lane curved to the right, leading straight toward a huge, two-story log house midway up the hill. Lemony lamplight shone from its many windows and gray smoke curled from several chimneys.

This was a prosperous home. She stared at it, mouth gaping open beneath her scarf, shocked. She was expecting a claim shanty, a small farmhouse at the most, but not this. In the distance, she spotted the hulking shadows of not one, but three huge barns.

"Our aunt is rich," Bea breathed in awe. "Do you really get to work here, Annie?"

"Y-yes." The word caught on her tongue, vibrated with astonishment. She blinked, and the house was still there, grand and beautiful. The back door opened, casting a fall of light on a big snowy porch. A slender, elegant looking woman draped in a wool coat raised one hand to shield her eyes from the snow as she peered at them.

Annie's heart thumped, knowing it was her aunt even before Adam pulled the horses to a stop. Her beautiful aunt, she realized as she got a better look. Even in middle age, the woman stood straight and tall, her heart-shaped face sweet with a timeless beauty.

"Why, who—?" Aunt Aumaleigh paused, then her blue eyes lit up. "You must be Annie?"

Love shone in that question, as surely as the lamplight shining, and Annie nodded, tears stinging her eyes. She felt wanted, such a precious feeling as she slipped out from beneath the blankets. She stumbled, hardly realizing Adam was already there to help her to the ground. Her knees were shaky, her legs unsteady.

"Welcome, child." Aunt Aumaleigh left the door wide open behind her, rushing across the snowy porch and flying down the steps, arms wide. Annie didn't remember taking a step, only suddenly being in the lady's slender arms, feeling her heart warm. The lonely places within her vanished.

They had family. Real family. Annie held on tight for just a second longer before letting go, stepping back to wipe her eyes.

Tears brimmed Aunt Aumaleigh's eyes too. Laughing gently, the lady swiped them away with the back of her hands.

"Goodness, what a surprise. I feared my letter didn't find you." Aunt Aumaleigh stopped, glanced at the young girl shyly standing back in the snow. "Why, who do we have here?"

"This is Bea." Annie held out a hand to grab her sister by the coat sleeve and tugged her close. "She's my little sister. She's fourteen, and she won't be any problem. I brought her along so we could stay together."

"Why, of course. Bea, you are just the best thing that could have come along." Their aunt drew the silent girl into a hug. Unmistakable caring pinched her face, a face that held a few haunting hints of their father—the cut of her chin, the high slash of her cheekbones and the color of her eyes.

Annie's throat closed up, with unexpected emotion.

"You two arriving here is the best gift I could have gotten," Aunt Aumaleigh declared, taking them both by one hand, just as kind in person as her letter had been. "And it's not even Christmas yet. Come in, come in. It's freezing out here. Let's get you warm and toasty. Have you girls had lunch yet?"

"No," Annie answered, glancing over her shoulder to where Adam stood, tall and forgotten in the snow, as substantial as one of those mountains in the background. She thought of all he'd done for them, agreeing to haul her things for such a small fee and loading them with care, showing up on time, well, early, after the stagecoach dropped them off and then, of course, his kindness toward Bea. Annie wished she could pay him what he was worth.

"Your driver is welcome too," their aunt stopped at the door to point through the storm. "You can leave your horses in the first barn. After we eat, we'll worry about unloading your wagon. Is that all right?"

"Yes, ma'am." Adam tipped his hat, his baritone booming with a manly strength and mightiness that made Annie's pulse trip a little.

Or maybe the man had no influence on her pulse rate and it was just hope rising up in her chest—the hope that everything would work out here. Encouraged, she followed their aunt and Bea through the doorway, into the beautiful house and into the bright lamplight. Bea's awe-laden "ooh" filled the air—the warm, delicious smelling air. Split pea soup must be in that kettle simmering on top of the large, fancy cook stove, set up against the wall nearest the door.

This one room was just for the kitchen, Annie realized as she unwound her scarf. Snow shifted to the floor, but she hardly noticed, taking in the beautifully crafted cabinets and the smooth stretch of counters. A work table sat in the center of the area. Crystal lamps cast plentiful light on two women wearing aprons over their dresses, busy at work making sandwiches.

"And just who is this?" An auburn haired, middle-aged woman asked as she slapped a thick slice of ham between two pieces of honey-brown bread. "Why, Aumaleigh, they look a little like you."

"Yes, Josslyn, they do." Aumaleigh blinked away tears as she helped Bea from her coat and hung it on a row of pegs on the wall. "These are my nieces, Eben's daughters, Bea and Annie."

"Oh, we weren't expecting two!" Josslyn set down her knife, wiped her hands on her white ruffled apron and rushed over. She cupped Bea's face with her hands, studying her intently with maternal warmth. "I knew your pa well. Always underfoot, that boy was. Aumaleigh, remember how we used to poke him with a stick so he would leave us alone in our tree fort?"

"I remember," Aumaleigh answered, as Annie hung her coat and scarf on one of the hooks. "Girls, I want you to meet my best friend, Josslyn. She's in charge of the kitchen. Louisa helps out here too."

"Hello, nice to meet you." The other woman looked up from slicing the ham and offered a shy smile. She had a dear face with apple cheeks and a rounded, carved chin. She was maybe in her late twenties, several years older than Annie was, but close enough that perhaps they could be friends one day.

Annie found herself smiling back. "It's nice to meet you too."

"Stomp the snow off your shoes," Aumaleigh said with a hold on Bea, "and I'll show you the rest of the house. We don't use it as a regular home anymore, not after your grandmother built the family home farther up on the hill. We use this place to cook and feed the legion of cowboys the ranch needs."

Annie checked her shoes before following her aunt and sister across the perfectly polished floor. Her soles squeaked, but she didn't leave any bits of snow as she wound her way past the women at the central table and into a small hallway. From there she could see a door to her left, clearly a small bedroom, the bed neatly made and personal items on the little bureau. To her right was a staircase leading up to the second story. Ahead of them was a large, beautiful parlor, where a fire raged in the hearth, making it so warm her fingertips began to tingle as they unthawed even more.

"Wow, it's really fancy," Bea breathed in wonder. "I've never been in a house this big before. It's almost as big as the orphanage, and there were forty of us there."

"Oh." Aumaleigh's face fell. She bit her lip, sadness robbing the brightness from her eyes as she laid a hand on the back of Bea's head and gave a loving stroke. "Had I known, I would have written sooner."

"We're grateful to be here." Annie felt shabby in her worn calico dress, the sensible brown color faded to a patchy tan in places. "I could really use a job. I hope there's still one available."

"Like I wrote, we always have room for family." Aumaleigh gestured toward the staircase, leading the way up. "We are short on rooms right now. Louisa has the bedroom off the kitchen and Orla has the only bedroom upstairs, but perhaps we can fit you into my office. We'll just move my things—"

"No, I don't want to inconvenience you." Annie hesitated, one foot on the bottom step. "We don't want to be an imposition. For now, we'd be happy with blankets on the floor in front of the fire."

"Oh, I think we can do better than that." Aumaleigh stubbornly kept going until she reached the narrow landing. She paused outside the first door. "Here is the room I had in mind for you, Annie, but I think we can fit Bea in here too. I noticed you brought some furniture?"

"Yes," Annie said, quietly. "It's not much, but I was able to hang onto it. I could have sold it, but I thought it might be more expensive to turn around and buy furniture here in Montana."

"True, although if you find yourself in need of a bureau or something, we can always ask up at the manor house." Aumaleigh stepped into the room. "Your cousins have furniture to spare."

"Cousins?" Bea brightened at that news, clamoring into the room.

"Yes, you have five cousins, Daisy, Magnolia, Verbena, Rose and Iris, and they are going to love you." Absolutely sure of it, Aumaleigh lit the lamp on the desk, aware of her nieces following behind her. They were both so shabby in those threadbare, worn dresses. What had they been through? It agonized her to wonder. Well, they were here and they were safe now. She was going to take very good care of them. "What do you think of the room?"

"It's nice." Bea glanced around, her braids whipping back and forth. "Annie, look at the big window."

"I see." Annie reached over and gently tugged one of Bea's braids. "Our bed should fit in here just fine."

Aumaleigh nodded, thinking the same thing. This room hadn't been a bedroom in a long time. "When the cowboys come in for lunch, I'll ask two of them to come move the desk and chairs out for us. We'll get you settled in here before you know it."

"Okay, I just really can't wait." Bea clasped her hands together, blue eyes gleaming. Nothing on earth could be more dear than that girl with her inner sweetness. "I love the room. Thank you, Aunt Aumaleigh."

"You're very welcome," she told the girl, who was far too thin, by the way, and her eyes full of too many shadows. An orphanage? That was not the place for one of her nieces. So thankful she'd found Annie's letter among her mother's things, Aumaleigh took the child by the hand and just held her. Love lit her right up. Oh, Bea was so young, just a sweetheart. Bea and Annie were not going to be alone anymore. "This used to be your father's room."

"Really? Pa?" Bea's blue eyes widened. Little sparkles of hope glittered there.

"Really. Eben was so funny back then." Aumaleigh's hand settled on her chest, where old memories ached. "He was always cheerful, just a jolly boy. Telling jokes, playing pranks, doing silly things."

"What things?" Bea wanted to know, her button face pinched, curious.

"Oh, he would steal my best bonnet and I'd look for it everywhere, thinking I'd misplaced it. Only to find him wearing it, the imp. He thought he was so hilarious." Aumaleigh laughed, the sweetness of that long ago time filling her. "He'd steal Ely's best Stetson too, waiting to see how long it would take for him to figure it out and tackle him for it."

"That's not the pa I remember," Annie said quietly, standing in the doorway, looking in. She was a willowy thing too, as if she'd also gone far too long without a good, square meal. "Mostly I remember him drunk."

"That is a sadness," Aumaleigh admitted, knowing what it was like to have someone let you down, to fail to be anything close to the definition of a good parent. Heart throbbing like a sore tooth, she wrapped her arms around her middle, not knowing what to say to the girls. Life had a way of changing a person, of stealing happiness and replacing it with despair. "Before Eben left, I caught him in Father's liquor cabinet. Our father drank away his sorrows, too."

"Aumaleigh!" Josslyn called from downstairs. "We've got the meal ready and I'm about to ring the bell."

"I'll be right down, thanks, Joss." Aumaleigh seemed to let go of the past with a sigh. She shrugged her straight shoulders, poised and elegant as she gestured toward the door. "I'd better get downstairs. When the cowboys descend, it's a free-for-all. Let's get you girls dished up first, or there likely won't be a scrap left. Those men eat anything and everything that isn't nailed down."

"Will I be helping out in the kitchen?" Annie dared to ask as she backed into the hallway, leading the way toward the stairs. "Or do you need help outside? I can learn barn work. I can learn anything."

"You'll be helping us with the house and the meals, Annie." Unmistakable love layered their aunt's words as her shoes tapped down the stairs behind them. "You'll be working directly under Josslyn and Orla, our maid. Come, you girls wash up at the sink, while I get two plates for you. I hope you like split pea soup."

"It smells heavenly," Annie answered, padding into the kitchen where Louisa hefted up a platter heaped high with thick, meaty sandwiches and left for the parlor. Annie watched her go, thinking it would be pleasant to work here among such friendly people. Including her aunt, who was just so kind. Unexpected tears burned behind her eyes as Aunt Aumaleigh herded them toward the wash basin. Already Josslyn had set aside two plates for them, both loaded with thick, delicious looking sandwiches.

Bea would have plenty to eat here. She would be safe and warm and happy. And they would be together. It was everything Annie had hoped for and much more than she ever expected. This felt like a place where they could belong. It felt as if they'd come home.

"Isn't it nice here, Annie?" Bea whispered, sidling in to give Annie's hand a squeeze.

"Yes, it surely is." The words caught in her throat, raspy with emotion. It was almost too much to believe. She gestured Bea to wash up first, pointing to the bar of soap. It was hard to believe something this nice could really happen for them.

But it had. Annie glanced over her shoulder, watching their kindly aunt at the stove, dishing up two bowls of soup for them. She was a beautiful woman with her sleek molasses-dark hair and classic features.

The door swung open, letting in the howling notes of the furious wind and a shower of snow. A man's muscled form emerged through the whiteness, taking on shape. Adam wrestled the door shut, his broad shoulders set, and immediately his gaze arrowed to hers. Those dark blue depths turned warm and dazzling. A hint of a smile eased into the corners of his chiseled mouth. He tipped his hat to her in silent greeting, and her stomach fluttered.

She tried to tell herself that her stomach did that because she was hungry, but that wasn't the case at all. The room seemed smaller and the air nonresistant as Adam shrugged off his coat, ambling closer to her.

"Here, Annie," Bea said, passing her the soap, giving her the perfect excuse to turn away.

But her senses stayed fine-tuned on him, on his heavy, easy-going step, on the deep timbre of his voice as he introduced himself to Aunt Aumaleigh, and to the solid, dependable feel of his presence that made her remember a time in her life when she'd been attracted to a man she thought was like that.

Never again, she thought, remembering Harold, remembering Baby Ginny and her heart receded, curling up like a dying flower.

"Are you okay?" Bea asked, handing over a prettily embroidered hand towel. Her light blue eyes squinted with worry.

"I'm just fine," Annie said, although it wasn't true. She would never be fine again.

CHAPTER FOUR

Adam dropped his rucksack on the wardrobe's lower shelf. The room they'd found for him in the bunkhouse was small, but at the end of the hall, so it was quiet. There were only two beds on opposite ends of the room. The mattress was clean and firm, and the linen nice quality. It was much better than a lot of places he slept, and as a teamster he was used to sleeping anywhere. Being this comfortable would be a welcome change.

"I hope you're settling in all right." A tall, dark-haired man stood in the hallway. He was Beckett Kincaid, the ranch's foreman. "The room isn't too cold for you? It's the farthest away from the stove, and I'm sorry about that."

"Not a worry." He shrugged, shouldered the wardrobe door shut and tossed his book on the quilt-covered bed. "I'm used to it."

"You're welcome to join us out front by the stove." Beckett had a friendly look to him, like he was a good guy and a fair man to work for. "The boys are starting up a game of poker. Aumaleigh sent us out a basket of sugar cookies."

"I never turn down a cookie." Adam took a glance around, making sure he had everything settled. "I'm a little rusty at poker. I probably shouldn't admit that."

"We all are," Beckett chuckled. "There isn't a lot of downtime on this ranch."

"Is it a big spread?" Adam joined Beckett in the hall, wanting to find out as much as he could about Annie's aunt and employer. He wanted to make sure she would be well cared for here. "It was hard to tell driving up in the storm."

"We're the biggest ranch in the county," Beckett explained, ambling along at a slow pace. Word had it he'd been severely injured not long ago, but he was clearly trying not to let it show. "We're expanding, so it's a good time for Annie to join us. I reckon Josslyn will keep her busy up at the kitchen house. It looks to me like you have a personal relationship with her."

"No, I just know her from back home." He sure hoped he sounded casual. His feelings for Annie were private and his alone. Plus, it was hard to tell if she felt anything for him at all. For a while there, he'd had a moment of hope, but during lunch at the crowded table full of talking and joking cowboys, he'd been separated from her. She'd eaten in the kitchen with Bea. He'd only caught a glimpse of her on his way out the door, when the meal was done. She had her back to him, washing dishes. She hadn't looked up when he'd passed by. He suspected that was a sign.

"I just want to make sure she'll do well here." He shrugged, not sure if he'd managed to be as offhand as he'd hoped. "She's had a hard time in Wyoming."

"We'll all look after her," Beckett promised with the sound of a man who meant what he said. "She'll be family to me soon. I'm marrying her cousin Daisy in less than a month."

"Congratulations." Adam had more questions but the hallway ended. The front room was full of cowboys, who called in greeting, waving him over. They were a good bunch, and it was a comfort to him. If he left without winning Annie's heart, then these men would be the ones looking out for her. (Not that he could bear the thought of leaving her.) He chose a chair next to an old, gruff looking cowboy and settled in. The heat from the stove radiated his way, and it felt good.

The door opened in a burst of snow and wind.

"Zane!" the cowboys chorused.

"Good to have you back," Beckett called out, pulling at a chair at the poker table. "How was your last job?"

"As quick as I could do it." The intimidating bear of a man shucked off his coat. Snow dripped off him. It looked as if he'd been driving out in the weather for a long while. "I hunted the outlaw down, threw him in chains and hauled him in as fast as the horses could go. I didn't waste time getting back home. You look better, Beckett. Good to see you on the job again."

"It's good to be back," Beckett answered, easing down into his chair. "Do you want me to deal you in?"

"No, I'm going to throw down my things and head back out." The man named Zane hefted a rucksack over his shoulder and hiked out of sight, leaving a trail of snow behind him melting on the wood floor.

"He's gonna go see that pretty filly of his." The gruff, old cowboy shook his head, like it was a sorry thing. "Poor misguided fool. He's gonna marry her, and then what? He'll be hobbled for the rest of his life."

"It beats hanging out in a bunkhouse for the rest of your days with a bunch of used up ranch hands," a younger man with reddish brown hair teased with a wink. He reached into his shirt pocket for a handful of change and tossed it on the table in front of him. Betting money. "Give me a sweet, pretty lady any day. I'd rather be married than living with the bunch of you, I'll tell you that."

"Ah, the ignorance of youth," a salt-and-pepper haired man quipped, eyes merry. "Don't be in a hurry to tie the knot, Shep. The best of us are too smart to marry."

"Or too ugly to attract a woman," a blond cowboy teased as he sorted through his handful of change. "I haven't ruled out marriage. Then again, unlike you, some women actually find me attractive."

More hoots and arguments broke out in a good-natured banter. Adam's gaze strayed to the window where the faintest glint of light shone from the kitchen across the yard, flashing now and then between gusts of wind-driven snow. Annie crept into his mind. He couldn't help but wonder what she was up to right now and how she was feeling. Was she glad to be getting settled in, maybe? Likely she was relieved to have landed in such a good place.

Then he saw a shadow move across the front of that flicker of light. Someone was outside the kitchen house. He glimpsed a woman's slender silhouette, her head bowed against the wind. His blood stalled in his chest. He'd know Annie anywhere. He was halfway to the door before he registered what he was doing.

"Where are you off to?" the gruff cowboy asked over the shuffling sound of cards.

"I'll join you all later." Adam grabbed his coat off a wall peg and stuffed his arms into the sleeves. "Something's come up."

"We'll keep a spot warm for you," the blond cowboy offered with a friendly air, turning his attention to the cards being dealt to him.

Adam grabbed his scarf and his Stetson, hiking out the door before he was fully buttoned. Wrapping his scarf around his neck, he stepped into the punch of the wind-driven snow. He didn't have to wonder where Annie had been going. There was only one structure she could be heading toward—the carriage house. He squinted through the snowfall, searching for her. There she was with her head down, flocked with white, doggedly plowing up the hill.

"Annie!" He cupped his mouth, shouting as loud as he could, but it was against the wind, and he feared she hadn't heard him. He tried again. "Annie!"

She whirled around, standing still. She was such a little thing, and his chest warmed, the heat of his blood overwhelming any sense of cold. Even the howling winds seemed to silence as he trudged toward her, his pulse thundering.

"Adam, what are you doing out here?" she asked when he was closer, her voice muffled by her scarf.

"That's what I was going to ask you, although I think I know." He navigated around so that he stayed between her and the wind. "You should be in where it's warm. If you need something brought in, I can do it."

"No, I want to see everything first." She took a step, hiking up and over a small drift. "I didn't get a chance to check and see how my things fared on the long trip."

She looked so frail bundled up against the storm, like a little wren lost in the snow and the fierce need to take care of her surged through him, growing ever stronger.

"Everything's fine. I checked them myself after I parked the wagon," he assured her, but he wasn't surprised when she walked a little faster, moving away from him. She did tend to be independent, but down deep he was afraid she would never see him at all, not really. That her feelings for him would never change. That he would always just be a stranger to her.

"I need to see for myself," she told him, blinking against the strike of snow in her eyes. "I just need to see them. I just—"

She didn't finish, but not even the icy wind could strip the emotion from her words. The few possessions she'd managed to hold onto were sentimental, reminders of loves lost. His gut cinched, hating all the sadness in her life. He plowed to a stop in front of her, blocking the snow and wind from touching her.

"Walk behind me," he said, helpless to do anything else. It's what he would always do, the only choice he could make, whether she knew it or not. "I'll break the path the rest of the way. This deep snow is hard going."

"Thanks, Adam." Her gratitude softened away the little crinkles of emotion tucked in the corners of her eyes. It was all he could see of her face because of her scarf.

Gratitude was something, he told himself as he plunged forward, up the sloping hill. It wasn't love, but it was a step in the right direction.

"Adam!" She shouted in alarm.

He heard a thud. By the time he turned around she was gone, sliding away from him, her skirts flying everywhere.

"Annie!" He lunged after her, afraid she'd hit hard and hurt herself, and terror drove him forward through the foot and a half of snowfall, especially when she stopped sliding and remained stretched out on her back, sprawled like a fallen doll. She raised her hands to her chest and... was she crying? *Was she hurt?* Adrenaline thundered through him as he raced closer.

"Oh, I'm such a klutz." She lifted her head off the snow to laugh up at him. "I can't believe I did that."

"Are you all right?" His pulse coursed through his veins so fast and hard he had to stop for a moment and take a deep breath.

"And here I'd almost gone a whole day without embarrassing myself." She shook her head. "I should have known it was too good to last. At least I didn't do it in front of my aunt, or she might worry what kind of person she'd hired."

"I won't tell her if you don't." He held out his hand, catching hers and pulling her onto her feet.

"I'm not sure I want you to know this about me either," she confessed, aware of how large his hand was covering hers before he let her go, how big and solid the man. Her stomach fluttered, and she was afraid to think about why. She had no excuses handy to explain it away. "I don't want anybody to know the truth about me."

"Too late," he teased amiably, tipping his hat to knock snow off the brim. "Don't think I didn't notice you walk off the end of the boardwalk one day back in Landville, and plummet straight to the ground."

"I do that a lot. I have a lot on my mind," she explained, her face heating beneath her scarf because, honestly, it was embarrassing. "Good thing I landed on my feet that time."

"It was a good save," he agreed, chuckling. It was a rich sound, like melted chocolate on a hot stove. Soothing.

Not that she should be noticing or thinking about him that way, she scolded herself. But it didn't change the fact that Adam Butler was remarkable.

"That day, I was driving by hauling hay for the McReady farm." He clarified, keeping pace with her as they retook the hill. "It had been a long, tough day, and I looked over and happened to catch sight of you walking straight off the boardwalk as if you didn't know it ended. I was impressed with how you hit the ground and just kept on walking as if you completely meant to do that."

"Practice," she told him, unable to explain away the warm feeling she felt in her chest as she walked with him. "If you do anything enough times, you're bound to get good at it."

She liked how he laughed, in an inviting, relaxed way. She didn't feel as embarrassed as she stopped to look at the evidence in the snow, where her body had left an impression when she'd slipped and she'd skidded down the slope.

"At least it was sort of fun," she confessed. "When I was sliding, anyway. It was almost like sledding."

"Seems to me you don't have much fun." He kept going, leading her into the lee of a wide, single story building lined with doors. The carriage house.

"I'm always working." She shrugged, glancing over her shoulder wistfully. "That doesn't leave time for much fun. Responsibilities come with work, not that I mind. Bea is worth it."

"Maybe it won't be quite as hard being here with your aunt." He hefted open one of the doors. "I'm surprised you're not working right now."

"I tried, but Aunt Aumaleigh caught me doing the dishes and shooed me away." A bubble of distress rose in her throat as she ambled into the shelter of the cold, echoing structure. Shadows looming in the darkness became wagons and buggies and sleighs when Adam lit a nearby lantern. "I wanted to start working this afternoon, but she said no. Bea and I should settle in first and I can start tomorrow."

"Good idea." He ambled away from her, fiddling with something that made a loud clunk when he released it. A big barrel lid, she realized. He turned to her, his grin wide and handsome, showing off a hint of dimples and even, white teeth. "Do you like your room?"

"Yes. It's the nicest place Bea and I have ever lived." She hesitated admitting where she'd been spending her nights before she'd left Landville. She'd been sneaking into the livery barn in town and sleeping in an empty stall, to save money so she could afford to get Bea out of the orphanage. That was the last thing she wanted Adam to know about her. Town gossip being what it was, he already knew most of the bad things about her. "While we were eating in the kitchen, Josslyn told me what she's paying for rent. There's a little shanty next door to her that's vacant, and it's close to the schoolhouse. Down the road, if I watch my money, I could afford something like that. It would be better for Bea to walk to school and have children around her own age."

"Sounds good to me." He handed her the grain lid, which was puzzling.

What did she need with a lid? But he didn't enlighten her. He ambled back into the shadows, fiddling with another barrel.

"Rumor has it that your aunt is paying you a decent wage," he said over his shoulder. "I'm glad. It looks like things have taken a good turn for you and Bea."

"Yes, it does," she agreed, tucking the lid under one arm. "It's hard to believe. It's almost too good to be true."

"Things are going to get better for you. It's okay to believe it." He appeared with another lid, his midnight blue eyes twinkling. "Come with me."

"I'm afraid to," she answered wryly, following him back out into the storm. Snow swirled down in fast, determined spirals, making the world beautiful. "I have a feeling I know what you're up to and it has nothing to do with checking on my things."

"This is a rare day off for you," he said, stealing the lid from her and setting it down on the snowy slope. "Maybe you should take a few moments to enjoy yourself. Remember what life is all about."

"I haven't gone sledding in ages," she confessed, but did that stop her from easing down onto the lid? Oh, no. She sat right down, heart pounding. "Not since I was a kid."

"Then it's time you had a little fun." He knelt beside her, so close she could see the smile in his eyes.

She didn't know why her heart gave a thump or why she reached out and laid her hand on his snowy scarf, right where his jaw would be. She could feel the solid iron of it through the wool.

Being this close to him, she felt calm and sure, as if all was right with the world. What was it about him that made her feel this way? She wondered about him, this quiet, industrious man whom she'd glimpsed around Landville driving his wagonload of goods through town or ambling down the boardwalk on errands. What was he like? What had he been through? He had to be in his late twenties. Why hadn't some woman scooped him up?

"Hold on tight." He leaned in closer, speaking against her ear. His warm breath tickled, fanning against the side of her cheek in a pleasant, thoroughly wonderful way. She'd never felt anything like the tingles scuttling across her skin as he sent her flying.

Down, down, down she went in a swish of speed and snow. The lid began to spin in a slow, twirling dance and she laughed, gliding along. "This is fun!"

He merely nodded in answer, standing at the top of the run, his metal lid tucked under one arm, watching her go. She shrieked, laughing as she glided down the slope.

"You should try it too!" she shouted merrily. "Don't just stand there!"

"I'm coming," he assured her. It was hard to move, she held him spellbound. She made a pretty picture with her skirts ruffling in a flash of brown calico, her black shoes shining starkly against the white and shadows. The end of her red scarf came free, a flash of bright color as she skidded from his sight.

It felt as if his heart was out there with her. He hunkered down on his lid, gave himself a mighty push and momentum shot him forward, down the slope. The snow was slick and he gained speed. Icy air chilled his nose, teared his eyes and cut straight through his layers of clothing. He held on, gliding faster in an exhilarating swoosh, soaring straight toward Annie. He could see her again. She was a sight with her blond hair streaming out behind her and escaping her knit hat. Her shriek of laughter held notes of joy.

He was riveted to her, enchanted. Suddenly she hurled up into the air, her barrel lid going one way and she going another. She soared through the air, laughing harder, flashing him a glimpse of woolen red petticoats and her white long johns. Then she was rolling. He didn't have a chance to see her land because he hit the same bump in the slope and was suddenly airborne. His lid went flying and he hit the snow, rolling to a stop on his back beside her.

"You did that with more coordination than I did," she told him as she blinked up at the snow, trying to catch her breath. "I shouldn't have done that. What if my aunt was looking out the window? She may be second-guessing her decision about now."

"Because you are lying here with your woolen underwear showing?" He swiped snow from his face, realized his hat had gone flying. No wonder his head was cold.

"That's part of it," she admitted, sitting up, a tousled and adorable mess. Her hat had flown off too, her scarf had come undone, her tidy blond up knot was askew. Golden tendrils curled down to frame her heart-shaped face. Her skirts were up around her knees, showing shapely and slender calves encased in woolen leggings. "I'm supposed to be an adult and here I am, playing like a child. You are a bad influence on me, Adam Butler."

"So I've been told," he quipped, sitting up. "I have that effect on all women. It's why I'm single at twenty-eight."

"Because no decent woman will have you?" She arched a slender brow, adorable as her face scrunched up in disbelief. She leaned over, stretching to reach for his hat. "No, I don't think that's the reason at all. Maybe it has something to do with your job. You must travel a lot."

"True, but if I were married, I'd take jobs closer to home." Truth be told, he'd concentrated on the higher paying ones, which usually involved distance. He'd been saving up as much as he could, hoping to marry one day. He wanted to give his wife the best life possible. His chest hurt with a painful love watching her brush snow off his Stetson. He cleared his throat. "I'm not married because I fell in love with someone four years ago, when I moved to Landville to work with my brother."

"You did?" She looked up, her sweet, beautiful blue eyes finding his. Innocent, she had no notion he was talking about her. "What happened?"

"She never noticed me." Being honest wasn't easy, but he did it anyway. He reached out and brushed a tangle of golden tendrils from her face, daring to touch her. His leather gloves grazed across her soft cheek, and his heart filled with longing. "I was shy back then, much worse than I am these days."

"I don't know, you're pretty shy. This is the most you've ever said to me." She tipped her head back when his fingers fell away, studying him intently, as if she'd never really seen him before. "You were nearly silent the entire drive from Deer Springs to here."

"It was cold," he reasoned. "Besides, once I get comfortable with someone, I'm not so shy. You may regret that. I might talk your ear off."

"That's okay. I have two of them, so I'll have one to spare." She went back to brushing snow off his hat. She must be cold with the wind hitting her, but instead of reaching for her hat, she concentrated on his. "So, you never spoke to the lady?"

"No, and I was too shy to do more than tip my hat to her if we met on the boardwalk." He took the Stetson when she offered it to him and plopped it on his head. "By the time I'd got up my nerve, some other guy started courting her. He was dashing and smart and I didn't think I had much of a chance. They got married, and that was that."

"I'm sorry, Adam." She stretched to grab her hat, turning away from him. For a moment, panic leaped through him, running fast and thick in his blood, fearing perhaps she'd guessed the truth. But when she turned around to him, giving her hat a good shake so the snow would fly off, she trained her poignant, soul-filled gaze on him. Only sympathy shone there. "I'm sure it was her loss."

His throat closed up at that, at the honesty low in her voice, in the way she nodded once with sincerity, meaning what she said. Now would be the time, he thought, the time to tell her the truth and let her know how he truly felt.

"Hey! Annie!" A child's voice called from down the hill, echoing through the noise of the storm. "How could you go sledding without me?"

"Oh, I was hoping you wouldn't find out!" Annie teased, shouting back, her laughter light and bright. Her happiness seemed to light up the shadows and he couldn't look away. There was no more beautiful sight than Annie like this, with her eyes sparkling and joy widening the smile on her rosy lips. She shone so bright that his heart simply tumbled, falling in love with her even more.

"Why don't I give my lid to Bea?" he offered, standing up, regretting that the moment was over and his chance had passed him by. Again. But there would be another. "Have some fun with your sister. I'll be in the carriage house when you're ready."

"Thanks, Adam." She beamed a smile up at him, and he hoped that something had changed between them in that moment before she turned away, calling to her sister.

Maybe one day soon, Annie would know just how devoted he was to her, that he was the one man on this earth who would never let her down. He stood, brushed snow off his denims and walked away, trekking up the hill. His step was light—as light as his heart.

CHAPTER FIVE

A dam. She couldn't get him out of her mind as she trudged up the hill again, listening to her sister's delighted squeals as she sped down the slope. Bea hit the bump and plummeted into the air, only to crash into the snow, laughing with glee. It had been a long time since she'd heard her baby sister laugh like that. Satisfaction ebbed in, chasing out every other thought. Annie turned around, walking backward through the storm, watching Bea bounce up. The girl was mantled with white.

"That was so fun!" she shouted, giving a little hop. "Now, where did my sled go?"

"Over there!" Annie called out, pointing toward the stand of tall, solemn evergreens. "I'm going to rest for a bit, okay? You've worn me out."

"I'm not done yet." Bea scampered across the hill, hardly hampered by the steadily drumming downpour of snow and the deep accumulation on the ground. "Don't stay away too long or I'm coming to get you and force you to sled some more with me."

"I knew you were going to say that." Annie spun around, chugging the rest of the way toward the carriage house, her breath rising in great clouds in the frigid air. She felt really happy, somehow even happier when Adam stepped into the doorway, so tall and strong.

Poor man, she thought, pulling down her scarf. He was all alone and unmarried. How could any woman not see what a good man he was? She thought of his story of love lost, how the woman he'd loved had married another. Sympathy pinched hard around her ribs, making it tough to breathe. She couldn't stand how easily love was lost in this world.

"I've uncovered everything for you." Adam greeted her with a shy smile. "I've set out all the crates so you can go through them. That'll make it easy to decide what to move and what to store."

"You did all this?" Her eyes went wide, taking in the few pieces of uncovered furniture in the back of the wagon box, the half dozen crates and boxes of items lined up neatly on the floor, their tops off. It was a thoughtful gesture, and guilt crept in. Honestly, this wasn't part of the bid he'd given her, but this was just who he was—someone who went beyond the call. He had a sturdy, solid, self-possessed sense of calm that made you think he was the kind of man who would and could do anything.

"I like staying busy," he shrugged, as if it was no big deal. "We seem to have that in common."

"Yes, we do." She rested a hand on the wooden sides of the wagon bed, gazing up at the furniture, some of which she hadn't seen in years, not since she'd been evicted from her shanty. The bed and bureau she'd grown up with, rickety and worn, but it was serviceable, but the rocking chair, that made her chest ache. Memories of those three days rocking fragile Ginny in that chair tortured her, and she closed her eyes.

"Perhaps I should have left that one covered." His male-hot presence came to a stop behind her. Sympathy rang in the low notes of his voice.

"No, it's okay," she assured him, squeezing her eyes shut to keep any tears from slipping out. She could cry forever if she let herself. "It's hard to remember, but it would be worse to forget."

"You should never forget." His hand lighted on her shoulder, radiating comfort. The heat of it seemed to seep into her, a balm to her broken heart, soothing her wounded spirit and she pressed into his touch. It was weakness, it was wrong she knew, but the years of loneliness and hardship and grief had worn her down, and when his arms came around her she didn't pull away. She let him draw her back against the steely plane of his chest, against his body's heat.

Oh, it felt good. She savored being wrapped in his strength, felt his chin come to a rest on the top of her knit hat, felt his calm strength fill her. The empty places within her no longer hurt and she no longer felt hollow as he gently rocked her. She no longer felt alone with his arms around her, crossed beneath her ribcage, locking her against him. She drank up the bliss of his comfort. If she let herself, she could let him hold her forever. When she opened her eyes, her tears didn't fall.

"Better?" he asked, his voice vibrating in his chest, rumbling through her.

"Yes. Thank you, Adam." She turned to face him, regretting that his arms released her, that he no longer held her against him. At least he didn't move away. He stood so close she could see the black flecks in his dark blue irises and see the individual stubble of his whiskers along his angled jaw.

"You're beautiful, do you know that?" His thumb grazed her chin, tipping her head back. His unguarded gaze searched hers, his pupils black and dilated, and his caring remained. "I don't think you do."

"I—" She hesitated, not sure if she should answer his question. Perhaps he didn't really want an answer because the way he looked at her made her pulse stammer. His gaze slid downward, focusing on her mouth, and she felt her lips soften, involuntarily parting as if they wanted his kiss—a kiss she could not have, a kiss she could not allow.

As he moved in, she planted the flat of her palm on the hard plane of his chest, stopping him. He did, not pushing her, but pain flashed across his eyes, pinching them in the corners, and he stepped back.

"I—" he began, perhaps to apologize, but Bea's clattering step interrupted. He had the decency to rear back, making it seem as if they hadn't been about to kiss as the girl bounded through the doorway, breathless, eyes sparkling.

"Annie, Aunt Aumaleigh is on her way!" Bea glowed, snow clinging to her so that she looked like a bubbly, happy snow girl. "I think she's coming to take a look at our furniture, to make sure it will fit in our room. Oh, it's really happening. We have a home together, and it's with family, Annie. Real family."

"I know, sweetie." Annie swiped at her eyes because those pesky tears had returned. The reality of Adam's near kiss weighed on her, and she felt part shame, part agony from a past she'd hoped to leave behind her in Landville.

She turned away from Adam, ashamed because she'd allowed herself to find comfort in him, when she had to be stronger than that.

She was a woman alone in the world, and that's the way it must stay. She was never going to trust another man with her heart, and, honestly, if the men in this town knew what Adam did about her, she wouldn't have to worry. She would be the same marked, dishonored woman here that she'd been in Wyoming.

So she turned her back on the man, no matter how nice Adam was, and held her arms out to Bea. She wrapped her sister in a hug, ignoring the cold radiating off her (not to mention the bits of snow), and turned her thoughts where they belonged—to her future, building a good life for Bea.

* * *

Well, that was a clear rejection. Adam had been wrestling down his feelings for hours now, but it wasn't working so well. His heart felt heavy as he manhandled his end of the newly filled straw mattress up the narrow stairs. His senses were fine-tuned to Annie. He could hear her dulcet, softly-spoken alto despite all the other sounds in the kitchen house. Conversations boomed around him, the stove door in the kitchen slammed with an iron *clank* and the knell of men's boots on the steps added to the noise.

"Just a little farther," Kellan, the blond cowboy, reported from the front end of the mattress as he glanced over his shoulder, backing up the steps. "It's gonna be a tight corner. Are you doing okay, Adam?"

"I'm good." His ears sharpened, taking in the lilt of Annie's voice behind him and the thump as she set one of the boxes down on one of the kitchen tables. "How about you?"

"It beats being out on horseback about now doing the evening feeding," the cowboy quipped, backing onto the landing. "But I can't lie. I'd rather be playing poker."

"You mean, losing at poker," the gruff cowboy joked, striding into sight. He grabbed one end of the mattress from Kellan. "You were losing anyway."

"I don't have a good poker face," Kellan told Adam. "I'm bad at bluffing."

"Me, too," Adam admitted ruefully, aware of Annie's soft voice in the kitchen behind him, feeling the murmur of her words brush over him as she spoke with her aunt. He winced, remembering her firm hand on his chest, blocking him from moving in for a kiss. That still hurt. He gritted his teeth, wishing the hurt would stay buried. She hadn't wanted his kiss, he'd gotten carried away by his feelings and now he'd lost his chance with her.

Maybe he'd known how this would end all along. Heart aching, he gritted his teeth, gave the mattress he carried a good heft, carrying it the last few steps and onto the landing.

"The angle is too narrow. We're gonna have to wedge it in there," Kellan decided, eyeing up the short distance to the room. "Burton, can you take over here? I'm heading back to help Adam shove."

"Sure thing." The gruff cowboy shouldered the weight of the mattress easily, holding it steady while Kellan squeezed along its length.

With a lot of muscle, a little patience and plenty of heaving, they managed to cram the mattress through the doorway and into the small room. It rested on the bedstead, set up in the corner, where Annie would be spending her nights from now on. He imagined her there, her golden curls fanning across a white pillowcase, asleep. He hadn't forgotten what it was like to hold her. She'd been soft and sweet, just the way he knew she would be.

"Thank you, guys." She hurried in, her arms full of bed linens. "I never could have gotten that up here by myself."

"That's what we're for, young lady." The gruff cowboy—Burton—tipped his hat courteously. "You need something moved or done, you let us know. Heaven knows Josslyn doesn't hesitate over any little thing."

"Hey, I heard that!" Josslyn shouted from down below in the kitchen, full of humor. "Watch what you say, or I'll burn your food."

"And she'll do it, too," Burton agreed, with a playful wink. "You'll treat us better than that, won't you, Miss Annie?"

"You can count on it." She set the neatly folded sheets on top of the bureau. "If I burn anything, it will totally be an accident."

"Uh oh," Kellan joked. "Aumaleigh, did you make sure she could cook before you hired her?"

"No, it was a risk I was willing to take," Aumaleigh answered cheerfully as she wrapped an arm around Bea. The pair stood in the hallway, side by side. "It was love at first sight with these two."

"You can't fight that," Kellan agreed with a shrug. "Well, since there's no more heavy lifting to do, I'll head out. I want to take a shot at winning my pennies back."

"Good luck with that," Burton grumbled, dimples flashing as he followed Kellan into the hallway and down the stairs.

"I don't need luck," Kellan teased. "I've got skill."

"Pretty poor skills, if you ask me," Burton drawled, their chuckles echoing from the kitchen below.

Adam sighed, realizing he was alone with Annie in the room. Feeling awkward and embarrassed over that failed kiss attempt (would he ever stop thinking about it?), he wondered what she must think of him. Not knowing what to say, he turned without a word and strode from the room. He felt the weight of her gaze on his back as he left.

He dug deep and found enough strength and pride not to look back.

Worse, the aunt gave him a sympathetic look as he passed her by in the hallway. It was easy to figure he hadn't hidden his feelings as well as he'd hoped. He tried not to listen to Annie's voice, a sweet lilting sound that wrapped around him and dug deep, as she spoke with her sister in the upstairs room, making plans and going about the business of moving in.

The kitchen smelled of the beef roast cooking in the oven and the doughy scent of rising bread. Hungry, his stomach grumbled as he headed toward the back door.

"A little something to tide you over." Josslyn held out a cloth-wrapped bundle. It smelled like sugar cookies.

"Much obliged, ma'am." He tipped his hat to her, wondering if she'd figured out the truth too. It was hard to say with the way she looked at him in her no-nonsense way, but he feared she had.

Great. What if everyone knew? With a sigh, he considered hitching up the horses and driving away, regardless of the roads. He could make it to Deer Springs and get a hotel room for the night, but with the heavy snow and the drifts it would be really rough on his team. He had good horses, and they didn't deserve to be worked that hard, especially not on their time off.

So it looked as if he was stuck here.

"See you in an hour for supper." Josslyn circled back to the stove to check on a pot boiling away on a burner. "Don't let those cookies spoil your appetite."

"No, ma'am." He stepped into the snowy downpour, glad for the shocking cold. It slammed against him, freezing him to the bone, giving him something else to feel aside from his embarrassed and pretty defeated heart.

"Adam, wait." Annie pounded down the steps, her skirts snapping around her slender ankles, the ruffled hem still damp from playing in the snow. His chest tightened, remembering her laughing and playing. She'd been as bright as that first day he'd spotted her on the boardwalk in Landville, coming out of the mercantile with a package in one hand and her hat in the other, capturing his heart without sense or reason.

He didn't want to talk to her. He wasn't sure his heart could take it. Standing in the storm, he debated it for a moment, but he couldn't walk out on Annie. He didn't have it in him. Regardless of how much it hurt, he stomped back into the entry way and closed the door against the wind and snow.

"Good, you heard me." She rushed up a little breathless, skidding to a stop in front of him. "I wasn't sure there for a moment. You and I need to talk."

"Okay." He gritted his teeth, felt the muscles in his jaw bunch as he braced himself. Surely this was about how he'd embarrassed himself today. Surely she wanted to talk about that almost kiss. Look at how much distance she put between them, which was hard to do in the little entry alcove. He steeled his spine. "Go ahead. Say what you have to say."

She bit her bottom lip, as if she were deciding the best way to break his heart all over again. Maybe she'd say she didn't feel anything for him, or maybe she'd let him down gently. Worse, she might give him a piece of her mind for having been so forward with her. Whatever it was, it couldn't be good.

"I was able to glance through most of my things." She bowed her head, studying the plank boards of the floor between them. "Everything made the journey perfectly. I know there were rain storms and hail storms and even snow, but nothing was wet or stained. You took such care with them."

"That's my job," he said gruffly, touched by her words. This wasn't what he'd expected. "Plus, I knew they were important to you. You've lost so much, Annie."

She lifted one slim shoulder in a shrug of acknowledgement saying nothing about it, but the sorrow darkening her blue eyes did. She didn't mention the little clothes and blankets she'd made for her baby, clearly lovingly folded and packed in one of the crates. She set her chin, as if determined to be strong. "It matters so much, Adam. Thank you. You must have checked your tarps often to make sure nothing was leaking."

"It was no trouble," he assured her, his words strained with emotion he didn't know how to name. It was a terrible mix of sad and sweet. He would never have Annie as his, but that didn't negate the power of what he felt. He would always want good things for her, and he'd do what he could for that outcome, anytime, anywhere. She had no idea how often he'd stopped to check the load, how many puddles of rain or layers of snow accumulating on the tarps he'd painstakingly removed. "I was just doing my job."

"I'm so grateful." She slipped her hand to her skirt pocket, pulling out a small fold of greenbacks. "It's the amount we agreed on. I wish I had more to give you, you deserve it."

He stared at the money she held out, and pain shot through him. It wasn't a quarter of what the trip should have earned him, and yet it was still too much. Too much by far.

"I can't take your money, Annie." He fisted his hands, fighting to keep the love he felt for her from his voice. He'd done the job out of love, not for money. "I know how difficult things have been for you. Keep it. Spend it on you and Bea. Get some new dresses so you can start your new beginning here right."

"I can't start it on stolen money." She raised her eyes to his and he didn't see love there. He saw the stubborn determination to do what was right—in this case, to pay what she owed him. Her eyebrows crooked and her forehead furrowed as if she were upset. "It's good of you, Adam, but this is yours. I need you to take it."

Oh, she had to go and use the word *need*. He would stop the world from spinning if she needed him to. He would hand over his life in an instant, for her. Frustrated, he blew out a breath and took the money, his dignity hurting right along with his broken heart. To her, this was just business, after all.

"Thank you," she said again, backing away, putting more distance between them. She tilted her head to one side, studying him with a furrow deep in her forehead. "Can I ask you something?"

"Sure." He shrugged, resigned. "What do you want to know?"

"About what happened in the carriage house—" She paused, staring at the floor again. "Were you forward with me b-because of Harold?"

The vulnerable hitch in her voice killed him. He felt sucker punched, as if the air had been beaten out of him. He'd never expected this. Remembering the man who had treated her so poorly, he couldn't hold back the affection in his voice. "No. It was foolishness on my part, but not disrespect."

"Oh." She didn't seem convinced, peering at him through her thick lashes. "Because after Harold left me, I had a lot of attention from men and none of it was complimentary."

"I'm sorry for that." Adam hung his head, defeated. He thought of Harold, the scoundrel, who'd married her at the Landville church. Except it hadn't been a real wedding and that lowlife left her pregnant and penniless, having drained her savings account on his way out of town. Adam worked his jaw, enraged, wanting to beat Harold bloody, and maybe any of those men who had been disrespectful to Annie.

"No," he finally said, his voice strangled. "I'm not like that. I think the world of you. Now, if you'll excuse me."

He ducked out the door before she could say anything more, like to let him down gently or tell him that she'd only allowed him to hold her in the carriage house because of her overwhelming grief for her lost baby.

The wind slammed into him, peppering him with blissfully cold snow, but it wasn't enough to numb him all the way through. His broken heart still beat, warm with love for her. He feared nothing, ever, was going to change that.

CHAPTER SIX

Annie stared at the closed door with astonishment, Adam's confession echoing in her ears. *I think the world of you.* His voice had boomed low, rumbling fondly and then he was gone, lost in the dark swirl of snow. Nothing could have shocked her more.

"Annie, there you are." Her aunt waltzed into sight, lovely in the lamplight. Her molasses-dark hair shone sleekly, soft tendrils curling around her heart-shaped face. Caring glimmered in eyes as blue as bluebonnets. "I just told Bea to get ready. She'll be down in a minute. Grab your coat. We are going out for supper."

"Out, where?" As far as she could see, there was nothing but snow and ranch land for a mile in any direction.

"I sent the stable boy up the hill with a note. Your cousins are expecting us for the evening meal." Aumaleigh brimmed with happiness—lovely smile and sparkling joy. "You are going to love your cousins. Verbena, the youngest, is your age. I think you two are going to hit it off. You two will be close in no time. Now, fetch your coat. The sleigh should be pulling up any second."

"Our cousins." Annie thought about that. Through the afternoon, Aumaleigh had casually spoken of the five McPhee girls several times, daughters to Uncle Ely, whom she'd never met. Nerves fluttered in her stomach. Family. That was a new concept for her, since it had only been her and Bea for years.

"Annie, did you hear?" Bea skipped down the steps with a clatter. "I've never been over to someone's house for supper before. It'll be like a party."

"Hmm, maybe we'd better reconsider, Aunt Aumaleigh." Playfully, Annie reached for Bea's coat, trying to move past her shock at Adam's confession. "Maybe Bea should stay here for supper."

"Do you think?" Their aunt arched a slender brow, mischievously. "Perhaps you're right. She's a little young for a dinner party."

"Very funny. I know you're teasing, you can't fool me." Bea skipped across the kitchen. "Aunt Aumaleigh?"

"Call me Aumaleigh, dear, just Aumaleigh. I'm afraid aunt makes me feel much older than I want to be." Aumaleigh took the coat Annie passed to her and held it for Bea to slip her arms into. "My only aunt was my grandmother's oldest sister, who lived with us when I was very small. She seemed ancient to me, maybe ninety years old. That was my only experience with an aunt, and I'm afraid even now when I hear that word, I think of an extremely old woman about ready to die. I'm not sure I feel comfortable with that. I'm old, true, but I'm not *that* old."

"Aumaleigh, then," Bea agreed, sticking her arms into her coat. "And you're not that old for an old lady."

"Why, thank you dear." Aumaleigh chuckled, although she winced at being called an old lady. While it was true, she was middle-aged, she was young at heart. "Oh, I hear Cal with the sleigh. Bundle up, let's not keep the horses waiting."

Annie buttoned her coat, trying to pay attention to the funny banter between Aumaleigh and Bea as Bea told of how she didn't intend to grow stodgy when she was as old as Aumaleigh. Annie wrapped her scarf around her head, her thoughts boomeranging right back to Adam. He thought well of her, did he? That really touched her.

She opened the door, her shoes crackling across the ice on the porch boards. She hardly noticed the wintry evening air or Bea tromping behind her because all she could think about was Adam's arms around her, holding her, offering simple human comfort. She'd clung to him because she'd been alone so long, and there was a part of her that would never stop hurting. It had been weak of her to accept it, but it mattered greatly that he understood.

Since the night Harold left her (he'd simply took the canning jar of her savings she'd hidden under the stove and walked out the door), she'd put a wall up between herself and men. Out of necessity, mostly, since that was when word spread around town about how her marriage wasn't legal (because Harold was already married, it turned out). Otherwise decent-seeming men began approaching her, treating her as if she was theirs for the taking.

But Adam didn't see her like that, and it meant everything. It put a spring in her step. It was easier to keep her chin up as she slipped onto the backseat of the sleigh.

"Here, Miss, this'll keep you warm," a youth's voice broke into her thoughts. Only then did she see the buffalo robes he was shaking out.

Before she could thank him, Bea hopped onto the seat next to her and took charge of the robes, making sure everyone was covered and snug. Heating irons on the floor chased away the chill as Aumaleigh leaned forward to speak with the young man.

"Thanks, Cal. We're settled and ready to go," she told him in a kind voice, one with a note of fondness. She clearly cared about the people who worked for her, and that meant something, too.

The team of horses bolted forward, their tails up, eager to get moving, pulling the sleigh uphill and past the spot where she and Bea had sledded earlier. They'd had a lot of fun, but it was her first run downhill with Adam that Annie remembered—how he'd leaned in to give her a mighty push that sent her flying downhill. A pleasant warmth settled in her chest. When she caught a glimpse of the lights from the bunkhouse through the snowfall, she thought of him. She wondered if he was thinking about her too.

"And that's Beckett's cottage," Aumaleigh was saying, pointing with a gloved forefinger farther up to the left. Lemony light spilled through a front bay window, although the storm made it hard to see much more. It was gone in a flash as the horses charged uphill.

"After their wedding this Christmas, Daisy will live there with Beckett. She'll be nice and close, which is a great comfort." Aumaleigh sighed happily. "You came at the perfect time, Annie. I suspect we'll be shorthanded with all the wedding preparation. The girls are sewing new dresses, and next week we are going to start cleaning McPhee Manor from stem to stern. Oh, look, there's the manor now."

Annie blinked snow from her eyelashes, gazing up at the faint silhouette of the shadowed structure. Tucked in a space in the trees, it was a Victorian with turrets and bay windows, with towers and gingerbread trim. The back door flew open and lamplight sparkled on the covered rounded porch, where a slender, brown-haired beauty tumbled out, draping a wool shawl over her shoulders.

"Oh! Aumaleigh." The woman laughed—a girl who looked about her own age, Annie thought, and wondered if this was her cousin Verbena. "I thought it might be Zane, although now that I think about it, he wouldn't have ridden up. Hey, Magnolia!" She shouted over her shoulder. "They're here!"

"Yay," answered a good-natured voice from inside the house. A willowy blond stepped into the doorway to get a good look. "Hello, there."

"Hi!" Bea called out enthusiastically. "I'm Bea, just so you know."

"Then come on in, Bea, and hurry up," the brunette called out, wrapping her shawl around her slender form more snuggly, teeth chattering. "It's like the arctic out here. Now, don't crowd them, Magnolia."

"I'm not crowding them, I'm just so excited," the blond answered breezily. "It's not every day you get new cousins."

That was just how she felt, too. Annie didn't remember getting out of the sleigh or crossing the snowy distance to the steps, but suddenly she was following Bea across the porch. Aumaleigh trailed behind, ushering them through the doorway. Annie stood in the warmth, blinking in the bright lamplight, surrounded by her cousins.

"Oh, you're just as dear as I imagined you'd be," Verbena said, hugging Bea. "Isn't she, Magnolia?"

"Yes, we're going to have to spoil you a lot, Bea," Magnolia said sweetly, as if she meant every word.

Annie felt her eyes sting, overcome.

"I'm Daisy." A slender, dark-haired woman took Annie by the hands. "It's so very good to meet you. I'm so glad you're here."

"Me too." She squeezed Daisy's hands gratefully, not quite able to believe this was happening. Wonderful things did not happen to her, they just didn't. And yet, this was perfect. Just like a dream—a dream of family.

"Let me take your coat," Magnolia said, a sweetheart of a woman, someone you just instantly liked. An engagement ring sparkled on her left ring finger, too. "I want to be the first to invite you to join us for Thanksgiving."

"Oh, Magnolia." The strawberry-blond cousin quietly stepped forward, shaking her head with a mockingly scolding gesture. "You beat me to it. I was going to do the inviting."

"I know, Iris, but I couldn't help myself," Magnolia winked, taking Annie's coat to hang it on the nearby coat tree. Bea's coat was already there. "I just got so excited."

"You *are* coming, right, Annie?" Iris asked. She was quiet and gentle, there was something about her that was simply dear. "We're all so excited about sharing the day with you and Bea."

"I would love that." It was the plain truth. She followed Iris through the spacious kitchen (a really beautiful, enormous kitchen). Bea was being shepherded out of the room by Verbena and Daisy. Delicious scents filled the air, coming from a few pots bubbling away on the fancy cook stove. "You have a beautiful home."

"Thanks, we moved in this summer, although living here while it's being renovated is challenging." Iris gestured toward the open glass door between rooms, where a stunning dining room came into view. A cozy fire crackled in a stone hearth. Annie caught her breath at the exquisite wallpaper and furnishings. She'd never seen anything as luxurious.

"But we're almost done with the construction," a sunny blond, who was pulling out a chair at the table for Bea, chimed in. "Hi, Annie, I'm Rose. It's so great that you're here. We'll have to take you on a tour so you can see the work we've had done. The end is in sight, and when it is done, I'll have my very own bedroom. I can't wait."

"Having your own room is something I highly recommend," Magnolia joked as she circled around to pull out the chair next to Bea. "Mainly because I don't get woken up in the middle of the night because someone put their cold feet on my leg."

"Hey, I thought you were the one with the cold feet," Rose joked.

"Me? No, you must be wrong." Magnolia laughed at that, tightening her grip on the chair she held. "Sit here, Annie. It's nice and close to the fire."

"Right next to me." Verbena plopped down in the nearby chair, at Annie's left side. It was such a snug feeling to be welcomed, as if she and Bea were very important indeed. Across the table, Aumaleigh watched all of her nieces with glistening eyes.

"I hope you like roast." Daisy swept into the room carrying a platter of perfectly browned, rich smelling beef. "Iris made the gravy and it's amazing."

"It is pretty good, if I say so myself," Iris agreed happily, setting a gravy boat on the table. Only then did Annie notice the food already there—a big bowl of fluffy mashed potatoes, a cloth-covered basket emitting the scent of warm sour dough bread, a serving dish heaped with green beans sprinkled with bacon bits, and a bowl of buttery creamed corn.

"Look, Annie." Bea leaned in to whisper. "It's so much food that we can't go hungry. It's like a feast."

"Yes, it is," she agreed quietly, aware of Aumaleigh watching them across the table.

Realization of exactly how hard it had been for them back in Landville crept into their aunt's caring eyes. Their cousins fell silent for a moment, as if they were thinking about that too. Annie didn't know what to say. She stared down at her lap, where she could plainly see a threadbare spot in the brown calico fabric.

"You have no idea how glad we are that you're here," Verbena said, reaching over to cover Annie's hand with hers. It was warm and caring, and Annie found herself blinking, unable to speak. Emotion had wedged like a lump of oatmeal in her throat, sticking there.

For the first time in a long while, it wasn't fear or desperation or loneliness she felt. It was hope. Real hope. The kind that overwhelmed you with its power, with its certainty. Looking around, she saw Bea's future. She saw happiness for her sister. Bea would spend her weekdays going to school, maybe her weekends visiting their cousins. These were people who already cared about Bea, Annie could read it in their expressions. That lump in her throat expanded until she could hardly breathe. This was beyond her wildest dreams. And it had come true.

* * *

"I have to confess," Aumaleigh said as she cut a small bite of angel food cake with her fork. "I was surprised that Zane took one more job. I thought his days of bounty hunting were over."

"It was one last job he'd promised to do," Verbena explained, shifting her dessert plate around to better attack her slice of cake. "He'd given his word and he didn't want to break it. Besides, he wanted to tie up loose ends and move his money from the bank in Helena to the one in Deer Springs."

"And he needed to find you an engagement ring," Magnolia chimed in from across the table, using her fork to punctuate her words. "And what a great ring it is, too."

"The biggest diamond I've ever seen," Rose spoke up, eyes shining with happiness for her sister. "Good job, Zane."

"I know, right?" Verbena held up her left hand to admire the exquisite square cut diamond that sparkled with all the colors of the rainbow. It was the most beautiful thing Annie had ever seen. Verbena sighed blissfully. "That man is one surprise after another. First he gave me the ring, then he told me about how he's made an appointment to look at houses in town tomorrow."

"I suppose he doesn't want to live in the bunkhouse forever." Aumaleigh lifted her fork to her mouth, hesitating. "Although he would be welcome to stay as long as he likes."

"He's comfortable on the ranch, but, well, I have some news." Verbena set down her fork, glancing around the table at her sisters as if she wasn't sure what their reaction would be. She bit her bottom lip, hesitating before she continued on. "Zane wants to get a house because we're getting married on Sunday."

"*What?*" the four sisters chorused together, the notes of surprise echoing loudly in the room.

"Married?" Magnolia arched one eyebrow, still shocked.

"On *Sunday?*" Iris arched two eyebrows.

"*This* Sunday?" Daisy shook her head as if that wasn't right, not at all. "You need more time than that. What about—"

"—dresses?" Rose interrupted. "We can't whip up something new by tomorrow. Sewing takes time. It just can't be done."

"Why the hurry?" Aumaleigh wanted to know, although she was beaming happy looks in Verbena's direction. "If you waited, we could go shopping in Deer Springs. You love the shops there."

"Yeah, they've got beautiful fancy dresses," Bea piped in, bouncing in her chair, likely overjoyed at the prospect of anyone actually getting to step foot inside one of those fine establishments. "And hats. And shoes."

"But I don't want to wait." Verbena's lovely face scrunched up apologetically. "Zane doesn't want to wait, and neither do I. We're in love, so we're getting married. Zane isn't the kind of man to waste time waiting."

"Why the hurry?" Annie asked timidly, not sure if it was her business to question Verbena's rush to the altar. Then again, it was what she had done and she'd lived to regret it every single moment of every day Harold had lived with her. "You should at least have time to plan, even if you want a simple ceremony."

"We're just so much in love." Verbena didn't seem upset by the question at all. Nor did she sound defensive. She had an aura of peace around her, one of absolute faith and certainty. "Zane has never had a real family and he's never known real love. Besides, I don't want to wait to be his wife. This feels right."

Annie nodded, not sure what to say. There were good men in this world, they may be few and far between, but she didn't doubt their existence. Adam flashed into her mind, and for one second she let herself remember how safe she'd felt in his strong arms.

"I just wish I had time to find a wedding dress." Verbena shrugged, taking a bite of cake. "But in the scheme of things, it's only a dress. It's the wedding that matters."

"I have something you could wear." Aumaleigh set down her fork with a clink. "Perhaps when you're in town, you can stop by my rooms and I'll show you."

"Aumaleigh, you have a wedding dress?" Magnolia asked, blue eyes wide with curiosity. "Ooh, you're going to have to tell us all about that."

"Well, it's a few decades old." Aumaleigh leaned back in her chair, studying the interested, beautiful faces of her nieces. All seven of them. Her heart filled, looking at them seated around her, her girls, her family. It made the sadness of her past love affair easier to talk about. "I wasn't always a spinster. I had a beau once and he was handsome. Kind. Strong. Gentle. And he proposed to me."

She watched Magnolia open her mouth, likely to ask what had gone wrong, but the girl stopped herself. The question hung in the air, as if everyone was wondering the same thing. Well, Aumaleigh thought, feeling the pain punch at her heart, that was best left for another day.

"Mother wanted to hire the best seamstress in the county to make my dress," she explained instead, remembering the joy of that time, when Gabriel had loved her. "Even though she didn't approve of the marriage, she had her standing in the community to think about. She wanted to throw a fine wedding so everyone would see how important and wealthy she was."

Aumaleigh stopped to shrug, sad for her mother and the empty way she'd lived her life. "She never understood when I bought the material and sewed it myself. I wanted it to be special, so I put love in with every stitch. All my hopes and dreams for my marriage to Gabe were in my heart every second I worked on that dress."

"You must have loved him so very much," Daisy said quietly. Compassion marked her face, made her even more lovely as she pushed a lock of molasses-brown hair out of her eyes. "A dress made with love and dreams is far better than the most expensive gown in the world."

"Exactly." Aumaleigh knew her niece understood, because Daisy had found the same kind of love that she'd known with Gabriel. The kind that came from deep in the heart, from one's very soul. Nothing could be truer. She skipped over her sadness and the devastating grief she'd felt when that love hadn't worked out. "Well, the wedding never happened and I tucked the dress away in one of my old trunks. I found it not long ago, and it's in perfect condition. Maybe Verbena would like to wear it?"

"I would love that." Verbena clasped her hands together, excited and overcome. "I can't believe you would offer it to me. I can't imagine a better dress than one stitched with your love."

"May it bring you your every dream." Aumaleigh heard her voice wobble. Refusing to remember that heartbreak, she lifted her chin, determined to concentrate only on the girls surrounding her—her nieces, now the new loves of her life.

"You still haven't said what the dress is like," Magnolia pointed out. "Curious minds want to know."

"Because you're thinking what I'm thinking," Daisy laughed as she took another bite of cake. "You want to borrow it too."

"Maybe. I mean, it's Aumaleigh's." Magnolia smiled, and when she did it was like the sunshine coming out from behind storm clouds, lighting up the world. "Our dear ma is gone, and Aumaleigh is the closest thing we have to a mother. You know we love you, right, Aumaleigh?"

"Right." And oh, how good it was to hear the words. Aumaleigh swiped her eyes. "I love you right back. Now, about the dress. It's made of white lawn that's soft as silk," she began, as Iris leaned forward to cut more slices from the cake and slipped Bea a second piece.

The fire crackled merrily in the hearth as the wind gusted outside, blowing with winter's fury. This time, when Aumaleigh recalled making the dress, she remembered more than the loss that followed. She remembered the girl she'd been, so full of dreams and love—unending, enduring, sweet, sweet love.

CHAPTER SEVEN

The faint clomp of horse hooves on the hard-packed road drew Aumaleigh's attention. She gasped, her pulse drumming with a rapid thud-thud-thud in her ears. Her palms went damp, and anticipation trilled through her like a song. Gabriel was coming.

When his team rounded the corner into sight, her world tipped on end. She drank in the sight of him, so perfect with his Stetson at an angle, the brim slashing down to hide half his face. She admired the amiable curve of his flawless smile and the wide set of his shoulders, sturdy and impressive beneath green muslin.

Gabriel.

"Hey, there." He pulled his horses to a stop with a light tug on the leather reins, drawing her attention to his large, capable hands. "What are you doing here? I figured I'd be picking you up at your house."

"I changed my mind." She hopped off the rail and landed in a patch of daisies. No way did she want Mother to lay eyes on this man, or she would send him packing so fast he'd be a blur racing down the lane. Meeting here on the main road was a much better idea. "Plus, I like to go for walks."

"Then that falls in line with my plans." He knuckled back his hat to get a better look at her. His gray gaze studied her intently, as if he found her far too fascinating and beautiful to look away.

Her heart fluttered, just rolled right over. No man had ever looked at her that way before.

"It's a nice afternoon for a drive." He leaned over to help her in. His palm was up, fingers relaxed, waiting for hers. "I thought we might stay in the buckboard for *a bit. Then maybe take a walk around the lake."*

"I'd like that." She smiled up at him and placed her hand in his. It was like touching a lightning bolt. White, dazzling energy charged through her, pure beauty, zipping through her like fate. When her gaze met his, she saw her destiny. She'd never believed in love at first sight, although she'd loved the romantic notion of it. But the moment her toes left the ground and she stepped up into the buckboard, it was as if her soul sighed with recognition, as if he were her one true match.

In a daze, she settled on the seat beside him, biting her bottom lip to keep from protesting when he slipped his hand from hers. The buzz of awareness remained, and that zing of connection in her soul did not relent. Instead, it changed her world. It made the grass greener, the flowers brighter, the sun incandescent.

Her skin tingled, aware of him on the seat beside her. Breathless, she watched him gather the leather reins, adjusting them capably in his hands. He squared his shoulders, but he didn't command the horses forward. Instead, he turned to her, his gaze on the floorboards at her feet. Only later would he confess the courage it had taken him, a shy man, to have come calling that day.

"You look beautiful." His baritone rumbled deep and almost bashful, but when his gaze found hers, she could see he meant every word.

The poor man, she thought. He must need glasses. But his inaccurate eyesight only made her like him more. No man would think to call a twenty-one-year-old spinster beautiful, and certainly not her. That was not a word she'd ever heard associated with her looks before.

"Thank you." She suddenly felt bashful too, aware of just how much she wanted this date to go well. Nervous, she smoothed a wrinkle in her yellow lawn dress, realizing that while he may be her destiny, he might get to know her and change his mind about her real fast. *"You have nice horses."*

"Thanks. They are good guys." As if overcoming his moment of shyness, Gabriel snapped the reins and the striking set of black horses took off at a friendly clip, their necks arched and their tails up. They looked like happy horses, simply enjoying their stroll through the countryside.

"The one closest to me is Stu, short for Stuart." Gabriel gestured toward the far black gelding who pricked his ears, recognizing his name, and listened in curiously as if to see what else was going to be said about him. Gabriel chuckled, his deep voice warming with clear affection. *"Stu is a good guy. He's a rule follower, does everything by the letter. If I forget something, like picking his hooves before leading him to his stall, he'll be the first to remind me. He likes order and organization. You'll never find him doing the wrong thing."*

"So if you were to let go of the reins, he wouldn't take off at a dead run?"

she asked, amused, as Stu shook his head, quite as if he understood human conversation. Maybe it was her imagination, but Stu's brown eye widened with shock and dismay, as if he would never be caught dead doing such a thing.

"No." Gabriel's laughter rumbled pleasantly. "Stu would sensibly trot along, trying to figure out what it is I would want him to do. But Sully, on the other hand..."

Sully, the horse directly in front of her, gave a toss of his mane as if he already knew what was about to be said and seemed quite proud of it.

"Sully is a character," Gabriel informed her. "You never know what he's going to do. He's not so much for rules and order. If you turn your back on him, he'll try and steal your hat. Yesterday, instead of standing like Stu did in his traces while I was loading the wagon, he reached out and grabbed my boss's wife's hat as she walked by. He tried to eat the silk flower sewn onto the band, and he wasn't even sorry for it."

"Good to know," Aumaleigh found herself laughing because Sully swung his head around to toss her a saucy look. "I'll guard my bonnet appropriately."

"And I'll help you with that." Gabriel's dark eyes glinted with humor and something else that was far more mesmerizing. "That's an awful pretty bonnet you've got there. My guess is that Sully will think so too."

"Is that true, Sully?" She asked the horse, who had turned his attention to the road, trotting along as if he were the most innocent horse in all the world. "Hmm, he looks like he's plotting something to me."

"Count on it. Yellow is his favorite color," Gabriel joked dryly.

"Mine, too. Next time I'll wear a different hat. What's the color he hates the most?" The question rolled off her tongue, as cheerful as the sunshine tumbling over her, and she realized what she'd said too late. Next time, as if she assumed there would be a second date. That was Gabriel's call, his decision, and it was still early. So far she hadn't said anything inane or embarrassing or something that would change his good opinion of her. She blushed, realizing how forward and presumptuous she was. Mother, if she'd overheard the conversation, would have been livid at her unladylike comment.

But Aumaleigh didn't know how to correct it.

"He doesn't like pink," Gabriel said easily, as if he hadn't noticed her gaffe. "He sees it and curls his lip. It's your best bet for next week."

The kindness as he said it touched her. He apparently didn't think her forward at all. He tipped his hat against the slant of the sun as the horses clomped around a curve in the road, bringing the lake into sight. Nestled in a meadow of wildflowers, glittering in the sunshine, it looked like the perfect spot for a lady's first date ever.

And maybe there was a chance he would keep on liking her, she thought, as he drew the horses off the country road. Stu and Sully pranced through the grasses growing over the lane to the lake. Butterflies bobbed by, larks sang and the sweet scent of the blooming wild roses filled the air. Aumaleigh's heart felt as light as those butterflies lilting through the air. She felt full of anticipation for what was to come.

"Here we are." Gabriel's deep voice held a warm, friendly note. Maybe that's why she liked the sound of it so much. He drew the horses to a stop, set the brake and held out his hand. His palm was wide and callused from hard work, his fingers long and well formed.

When she laid her hand on his, she was prepared this time for the lightning bolt charging through her, a sensation that was as emotional as it was physical. Her heart opened, exposing places within she'd never known were there—a larger capacity to love and for love to fill. She slid across the cushioned seat until she reached the end.

When she stood, he reached up for her. Instead of simply helping her down, he lifted her. He was a big man, all strength and brawn, but there was something infinitely tender in the way he lowered her slowly to the ground. His dark eyes, a charcoal gray, fastened on hers and her heart stopped. It ceased beating right there in her chest, and she would have thought she'd died except for the fact that she was breathing, that her toes touched the ground lightly and she was standing on her own, gazing into his gray depths and feeling wholly alive for the first time.

"I'm so glad you said yes to me." He flushed, turning pink around the edges, his chiseled mouth twisting up into a sheepish grin. "I saw you and I thought, I don't have a chance."

"Oh, now I know the truth about you. You are a charmer. You're one of those dandies, aren't you?" Not that she believed it for a second, not with Gabriel's steadiness and sincerity. He looked like the kind of man who would never let anyone down. But it was the only explanation for his flattery. "You have women falling at your feet."

"It's true, I confess it." The joke twinkled in his eyes, where light gray flecks gleamed like polished silver. "I'm a reformed rake, but when I saw you I couldn't help myself. I went back to my old ways."

"Right." She rolled her eyes, smiling. His smile joined hers and it was a strange and wonderful sensation. She was shy, never knowing what to say to men, but here she was bantering with Gabriel. He just felt so right. "You don't have to flatter me. I'd like it better if you didn't."

"I'm not flattering you." He blushed faintly again, in the most endearing way. "I'm simply telling the truth. I'm not at all sure why a lady like you is here with *me."*

"*A lady like me?*" She arched her brows, scrunching up her forehead in surprise and bewilderment. "*What does that mean?*"

"*Well, you live in a fancy house. Your parents are wealthy.*" He gave a humble shrug of his wide shoulders. "*Surely you could have better suitors.*"

"*Not in my opinion.*" Her face heated. There she went, being forward again. She stared down, focusing on the toes of his boots, polished black leather against the vivid green wild grasses.

"*I'm glad to hear that.*" His forefinger caught her chin, nudging it up until her gaze met his. Kindness shone there, deep and true. "*I'm very glad.*"

He brushed a lock of her hair out of her eyes, tucking it behind her ear. He had the capacity for amazing tenderness, and in that moment she knew she wanted him forever. She wanted to be treated just like this, with his awkward affection, with that compelling, adoring look in his gray eyes.

Don't mess this up, she told herself, letting him take her by the hand. She never wanted him to stop looking at her that way.

Without another word, he led her past the horses. Stu lifted his head from grazing, and with a dandelion hanging from between his horsy teeth, he gave her a gentlemanly nod. Sully strained against his traces, his eyes on her hat.

CHAPTER EIGHT

I n the warmth and light of the early morning kitchen house, Annie dealt out plates from the stack tucked in her arm, settling them neatly in front of each chair in the parlor/dining room. The windows let in a weak gray light and gave view to a snow-mantled world. Everywhere she looked was pure, sugary white—the sloping hill, the reaching meadows and the half-hidden mountains, their peaks lost in the storm clouds. Snow fell in giant, determined flakes straight to the ground. She didn't know how Adam would easily make his way out today.

Footsteps tapped in the hallway, coming closer. Josslyn, in a gray dress, a ruffled apron with her auburn hair tied up in a soft bun swept into the room with a pitcher in each hand—one of milk and one of water. She set them on the edge of the table.

"It's handy having you here, love," she said, nodding in approval as she noted the plates, cups and the tidy silverware laid out and glinting in the lamplight. "You've saved me many a step already this morning. You're a fast worker too."

"I'm grateful for the job." She set the last plate down at the head of the table. It had to be a challenging job, feeding dozens of cowboys. It felt good to know she was making Josslyn's workload lighter. "What do you need me to do next?"

"Come back to the kitchen with me. Louisa is ringing the bell right now," Josslyn paused, tilting her head to listen to the clanging, muffled by the walls. "They ought to be descending any minute. You saw what it was like last night. That horde of men will eat anything they can get their hands on. Come help me bring in the platters before they do or they'll be restless. And one thing you don't want is a bunch of hungry, restless cowboys."

"I'll try to remember that." Annie matched Josslyn's quick pace as she race-walked down the hallway. Was it wrong that the instant she heard men's boots in the doorway, she wanted it to be Adam? He had been so kind to her. Inexplicably, the center of her chest warmed, brightening when she thought of him.

"Take those boots off," Josslyn ordered to one of the cowboys, handing a platter of bacon to Annie and waving her in the direction of the table. Stern, that voice, but her eyes sparkled with good humor. "You walk across my clean floor in snowy boots, and you'll be mopping it to a shine. Mark my words."

"Yes, ma'am." One of the younger cowboys tipped his hat to her, stepping back onto the entry mat. He sat down on a nearby bench and yanked off his boots.

No sign of Adam yet. Annie swished down the hall, resisting the urge to glance over her shoulder to watch for him. She shouldn't be so interested in him, she told herself as she set the platter in the center of the table. When she whirled around, Josslyn stood behind her, handing her two more platters. Steam rose from hash browned potatoes and scrambled eggs and her stomach rumbled as she set the platters on the table.

Adam had been on her mind last night too during the late quiet hours. After supper, she'd hugged her cousins goodbye, ridden home with Bea and Aumaleigh and tucked Bea into bed. Sleep had eluded her as she'd lain beside her sister, staring at the dark ceiling. She couldn't put her finger on it, but something bothered her about Adam. There was something she should have noticed about him.

Or, maybe she was just in turmoil because she liked the way he'd comforted her, holding her in his arms. Long ago she used to dream of being held like that—safe and secure. Once, she'd dreamed of a good, kind man, one who would protect her and love her more than his life.

Harold had shattered that dream. She wished there was a way to piece that dream together again.

Louisa sailed in with two big baskets of biscuits in her arms. She gave a friendly smile, but there was no time to talk. Men were crowding down the hallway and into the room, looking hungry.

"Hmm, that sure smells good, ladies." Kellan, blond and strapping, moseyed in. His gaze zipped straight to the table and he grinned wide. "Thanks for scrambling the eggs, Joss. You know I like 'em that way."

"Just so you know, I didn't do it for you," Josslyn called out on her way back to the kitchen, her words laced with humor. "That's not why I made those biscuits you like either."

"It is too." Amused, Kellan drew out a chair and folded his big frame into it. "You know I'm your favorite."

"No, Shep is," Josslyn argued lightly. Clearly it was an old joke between them.

The men clamoring into the room laughed, ribbing Shep for being the favorite ("I'm not," he argued good-naturedly, "or she would have made pancakes").

As soon as the hall was clear, Annie slipped away, hurrying to the kitchen. There was Adam, sitting on the bench, pulling off his left boot. He stiffened, as if he sensed her presence, and when he looked up, his gaze brightened, just for one moment, before he looked away and intently sat his boot on the floor.

"Good morning, Annie." He reached to haul off his right one. He looked a little flushed across his high, chiseled cheekbones.

"Good morning." His last words came back to her, ringing in her memory. *I think the world of you.* It mattered what he thought of her, more than she realized. As she stood there, in the kitchen with Louisa carrying plates to the little oak table next to the window and Josslyn fetching two more plates from the warmer, it struck her what had been bothering her about Adam.

He'd tried to kiss her yesterday, and if he wasn't taking liberties with her, if he didn't think her a woman with low morals, then what had it meant? Did Adam like her? Or had he simply been carried away by the moment?

Footsteps pounded down the staircase behind her, ringing with child-like enthusiasm. Bea.

"Annie!" The girl burst into the kitchen, her red calico dress snapping and her blond braids bobbing. "I'm up and ready and everything. Can you believe it?"

"No. I'm about to drop from total and complete shock." She tried to force her gaze away from Adam, but she couldn't. Her eyes stayed trained on him, noticing the muscles rippling beneath his blue flannel shirt, the dark swirl of hair at the back of his head as he turned to set his boot with its mate. How he rose from the bench to his tall, towering height. The sight of him as he moved toward her through the room made her stomach drop in one slow, giddy swoop.

"I'm usually a sleepyhead," Bea explained as she dashed over to the little kitchen table by the window. "But not this morning. Last night, Aumaleigh said I should start school today. Do you think with all the snow that it will be open?"

"Of course it will," Josslyn answered. "An education is a privilege. It's not a blizzard out there, so a little bit of snow won't get in the way of that."

"A little bit of snow?" Bea laughed, pulling out her chair at the table. "There's tons of snow out there."

Annie couldn't hear what Josslyn said in response because her mind had gone complete and utterly blank. Her brain refused to function as Adam strode her way, his gaze fastening on hers and holding there, refusing to leave. Sweat broke out on her palms and the back of her neck. Her pulse went crazy, thundering in her ears.

"But Annie doesn't know how to drive," Bea was saying somewhere in the background as if from a far, far distance.

"I'll drive you," Adam said, stopping in front of her. "If that's all right with Annie?"

"Uh—" She opened her mouth without knowing what she intended to say. Her first thought was no, because he'd wanted to kiss her. Or yes...because he'd *wanted* to kiss her. She felt as if she stood on the edge of a precipice, feeling the ground beginning to crumble at her feet and there was no escape, nothing to do but tumble all the way to the ground. "Adam, aren't you leaving today?"

"The guys said the roads will be tough going with those high winds we had last night. I don't want to work my horses that hard, having them struggling with deep drifts. Especially when the road will be better in a day or two." Adam shrugged, drawing her attention to the curve of his muscled shoulders and the breadth of his chest.

She remembered being held in his arms, being tucked against that chest. Part of her wanted to be there again.

"I'd be happy to take you both," Adam added with a nod, certain, his tone leaving no doubt. "I'm assuming Annie will want to meet your new teacher."

"Annie says yes," Bea answered confidently. "Don't you, Annie?"

"Uh—" Did Adam like her, she wondered? Was it even possible that he cared for her romantically? The thought left her bewildered. "Sure?"

"You don't sound sure about that." Adam stood there composed, mighty with the lamplight shining nearly black in his hair, flashing a calm half-smile.

"She's sure," Bea insisted above the scrape of two more chairs on the hardwood—the sounds of Louisa and Josslyn sitting down at the kitchen table to eat.

"Okay, then. I'll hitch up after I'm done with breakfast." Adam promised with a manly chin jut. With a nod of parting, he strode off, passing her by without another look, but she turned to watch him disappear into the next room.

She should have said no, she thought. Definitely, she should have said no.

* * *

A little while later, snow still tumbled from the sky as Adam knelt to tighten the last buckle of the rigging. His horses were stabled nearby, watching him as he rose and patted one of the ranch horses on the flank.

"Phil's a good horse." Beckett gave the black gelding a pat on the nose. "He's used to winter driving around here, and he knows the route. He'll be the horse Annie will be taking to and from town, most likely, so it's good she gets used to him."

"I'll help her with that," Adam promised, remembering how unsure she'd been about having him along this morning. It had been Bea who'd wanted him to drive them, not Annie. No, Annie had hardly been able to say more than a few words to him, mostly about if he would be leaving today.

That wasn't easy on his heart, but it didn't matter. This was about her. Always, it was about her. She was what mattered, not him.

"Good," Beckett said, nodding in the direction of the kitchen house. "I'll be taking my daughter in a bit. You could follow me, if you wanted to wait."

"I think Annie wants to go early and talk with the teacher."

"I see. Well, the schoolhouse is easy to find. It's on Second Street, not too far from the lumberyard. Just aim for the bell tower."

"I can manage that." Adam tipped his hat to Beckett, climbed into the sleigh and shook out the buffalo robes. The heating irons he'd placed on the floor had chased away the worst of the chill, so he covered the seats, to trap in the hot air and took up the reins.

Phil was an easy-going horse, lurching forward at a sedate pace, drawing them out of the barn and into the beat of the falling snow. It was hard to see the light from the windows through the downpour, but when he stopped the horse in front of the porch, there was Annie, watching for him. His chest twisted painfully, seeing her beauty, her sweetness. She was bundled in her brown coat and red scarf. Her hood hid her hair from sight, but a wayward tendril had fallen from beneath her hat to curl against the soft curve of her pink cheek.

Without a word, she closed the door behind Bea and herded the girl across the porch. He climbed off the seat and stood in the snow, waiting as Bea waded down the steps. She had a small silver lunch pail in hand.

"Thanks for taking me to school." She beamed a smile at him. "You're my favorite driver, you know, on account of we know you."

"That makes good sense," he told her, holding up the buffalo robe for her. "You already know I'm not prone to driving into ditches or falling asleep at the reins."

"Exactly." Bea scooted across the seat, huddling beneath the blankets. "How come we aren't taking one of your horses?"

"It's good for them to rest between jobs," he explained, feeling Annie getting closer even without turning around. The back of his neck tingled, and his heart beat quicker at the soft pad of her shoes on the steps. "Besides, Annie is going to need to learn to drive, so why not start with the horse she will be taking to and from town?"

"I heard that," Annie said, trudging to a stop in the snow beside him. She smelled like vanilla and snow, and when she turned to him, anxiety shadowed her light blue eyes. "I'm grateful for this job, but believe me, I'm not sure I want to drive a horse. We're so remote out here, it's clearly necessary, but—"

"No buts and no worries." He held the buffalo robe for her, tenderness coursing through him, sweet in his blood. It had been amazing holding her, and a newer, stronger tenderness came to life in his chest. He gestured to the horse. "This is Phil. I hear he's a great guy. Isn't that right, Phil?"

The big black gelding stomped one rear hoof and gave a low-throated nicker. He arched his neck, as if there was no doubt about it. There wasn't a finer horse anywhere.

"See? He's friendly," Adam assured her, unable to fight the way he felt.

"Hi, Phil." Annie gave a little wave. "It's good to meet you."

Phil swiveled his ears, taking in the sound of her voice. He gave another amiable nicker, presumably one of greeting.

Adam knocked snow off his hat, waiting for Annie to get settled. She didn't look at him in that knowing way women had when they liked you. She didn't bat her eyelashes or give him a shy smile. Instead, she slid carefully into the exact middle of the seat and took the buffalo robe from him, patting it snugly around her and Bea.

Disappointed wasn't the word, but he respected her feelings, even if they weren't what he'd been wishing for. Ignoring the ache in his heart, he eased onto the seat beside her and held out the reins to her.

"You drive," he said with a head nod to show his confidence in her. "Go on, it will be fine. Phil will be a perfect gentleman, won't you Phil?"

Phil nodded enthusiastically.

"See? You have nothing to worry about." Adam put the reins into her hands—so small, so feminine. He ignored the bright awareness he felt whenever they touched. It was bittersweet being this close to her—sad because she did not love him, sweet because he was spending time with her.

"Okay, I can do this," Annie said more to herself than anyone as she took charge of the thick leather straps. She turned her attention to the horse standing with his ears swiveled, head up and at the ready, eager for her first command. "I just shake them, right?"

"Just a gentle snap," Adam confirmed, leaning in to take the reins, his gloves grasping the leather straps a few inches in front of her hands. "Like this. It doesn't take much. See?"

He gave the reins a small shake, and Phil took off at a slow walk, his steeled shoes clinking on the hard packed snow. He released his grip. "You're driving. How does it feel?"

"Strange. It's not as worrying as I thought." Annie sounded more confident so he leaned back and away from her, careful so that his arm didn't bump her shoulder. "Horses are so big, I'm usually glad other people are the ones trying to control them, but look. Phil took the corner all by himself."

"He knows we're heading to town." Adam relaxed against the cushioned seat, listening to the squeak of the sleigh's runners on the snow and rubbed snow out of his eyes. "It's hard to see anything in this storm, much less the school's bell tower. Let's hope Phil knows the way there, too."

Phil swiveled one ear in their direction and nickered low in his throat, as if to say in his horsy way, "Of course."

Apparently, Annie wouldn't need to drive Phil as much as to simply tell him where she wanted to go.

"Oh, this is thrilling." Although her face was covered by her scarf, her eyes sparkled with joy. She'd never looked so alive. "I never expected it to be like this. It's like I can feel him through the reins. Oh, he's turning onto the road."

"Then tug lightly with your left hand," Adam advised wryly, "although it's customary to rein him before he turns."

"I'll work on that," Annie said with a laugh, as Phil wisely spotted previous tracks in the snow and followed them, so it would be easier going for all of them.

The sleigh skidded along, rising and falling over small drifts, weaving around taller ones. The world was hushed and still, except for the thousand *tap, tap, taps* of snow falling everywhere. The wintry world was frozen but stunning, and with one look at the condition of the roads, Adam was glad he'd decided to spare his horses the work of fighting through this all the way to Deer Springs.

"Annie, you're driving really good," Bea said, her voice muffled by her scarf. "Isn't this like a dream? I get to go to school like regular kids."

"You are a regular kid, Bea, except wonderful in every way." Annie's words dipped with affection, warm and loving.

He'd never heard anything as beautiful. Adam tucked the buffalo robe more tightly around him, since the wind was gusting. He would give anything to hear her speak to him like that.

"No, Annie," Bea argued. "That's you, wonderful in every way."

"What's wonderful is Aumaleigh," Annie said, dismissing the compliment Bea paid her. "She's so good to us. It's almost hard to believe."

"Believe it," he told her. He cleared his throat, careful to keep his emotions out of his voice, although he sounded overly gruff. "You're going to have to get used to having family around who cares for you. It's just that simple."

"Right, well, it's a lot to take in." Her voice dipped, and she felt open to him, as if the protective safeguards around her heart had eased down, letting her wounded places show. "Good things don't happen to me."

"Then it's about time they do."

"Every time I think things have changed, that something good has come my way and it will be different now, I've been wrong." Annie took her gaze off the horse and the road, her light blue eyes fixing on him. "I'm almost afraid to believe that what we've found here will last. It's too good to be true."

Compassion shone there, and so did a touch of sympathy, as if he hadn't hidden his emotions as well as he'd thought. It troubled him, because he didn't think she was speaking only about her good fortune here. It felt personal, as if she'd pushed him away.

"Sometimes what's too good to be true can last forever," he said gently, resisting the urge to take her into his arms again and hold her until she believed in all the goodness he wanted for her. "Your aunt loves you. Nothing is going to change that, not your past, not anything. It's going to be okay for you. Trust in that."

"Thanks, Adam." Her eyes turned luminous, full of hope and showing those wounds scarring her heart. Those scars were the reason she couldn't care for him in a deep way.

He gave her an awkward smile and stared straight ahead as the town of Bluebell came into sight. He blinked at the snow getting in his eyes, wishing he had a heart of stone so he couldn't feel anything, not this crushing pain of knowing he'd lost her, not anything ever again.

CHAPTER NINE

The schoolhouse sat on the last block on the second street of town, nearly hidden by the steady veil of falling snow. When Phil brought them to a stop (only after he had halted did Annie remember to draw back on the reins), the building looked ghostly, white against the snow. That is, except for the golden light from the two windows that faced the road. Gray smoke curled from the stovepipe. Although it was early for school, the teacher was in, readying the building for the children who would be coming through the cold storm.

"I'm sorta really nervous." Bea's voice sounded thin and shaky as she stared up at the schoolhouse. "I haven't been to a real school in a long time."

"It will be fine." Annie only wished she had money to buy a slate for Bea, but it would have to wait until her first payday. She patted Bea's hand beneath the buffalo robes, hoping she could will comfort and courage through her touch. "Remember how during supper last night our cousins said all those glowing things about your teacher? They are friends with her, so she must be nice, right?"

"Right." Bea drew in a breath, trembling a little, poor thing. She set her chin, determined. "Okay, I can go in now. Will you come with me?"

"That was my plan all along." Annie tugged away the buffalo robe to make it easier for Bea to climb out. The icy weather cut like a knife to the bone. As she scooted out after her sister, she felt Adam's gaze on her, felt aware of his presence.

"I don't want to make you wait," she told him quietly, afraid to meet his gaze because she was leery of what she would find there. It wasn't easy to see his deep regard for her. It made her remember how snug and safe she'd felt in his arms. She could not let that sweet moment sway her. "I promise to be as quick as I can."

"It's okay, take your time." Patient and understanding, he rose from the sleigh too. On the other side of the vehicle, he reached into the back. "I'll blanket Phil so he's not standing in the cold. I'll be waiting right here."

"Not half frozen, I hope," she teased, not daring to look at him. She didn't want him to misconstrue her concern for him as anything more than what it was—for what it could never be. She took Bea by the shoulder, forcing her feet forward and away from him, although it felt as if something held her back. Her chest ached in an unexplained way, so she tried not to think of Adam standing alone in the snow. She would be smart not to think of Adam at all.

"What if no one likes me?" Bea whispered as she climbed the steps slowly, her feet dragging. Her fears had taken hold. "What if I'm so far behind everyone thinks I'm dumb?"

"You are not dumb and don't you ever forget it. You are the smartest girl I know." Annie slipped one arm around her little sister (she was trembling hard) and opened the door.

Warmth greeted them along with the cheery glow of lamplight. Annie nudged Bea forward through the doorway and followed her in, drawing the door closed behind them. She stood there, dripping snow, in a wide vestibule full of empty shelves and hooks where the students would put their coats and things.

"Go ahead and take off your wraps," Annie advised, unwrapping her scarf. She took Bea's lunch pail and plunked it neatly on the nearest shelf. "Then we'll go in and meet your new t—"

But the teacher appeared, interrupting her, standing in the vestibule with a surprised but welcoming smile.

"Why, hello there," she said in a quiet, comforting voice. "I'm Penelope Shalvis, and I'm so glad you're here. It's always wonderful to get a new student. You must be Bea."

"How did you know?" The girl unwrapped her scarf. She'd gone completely pale with no sign of her usual exuberance.

"News travels fast in a town this small," the teacher answered kindly. "Besides, I know your cousins very well."

"Oh." Bea looked a little less nervous. "This is my sister, Annie. We had to come early to talk to you because I'm...b-behind."

"Well, I've had students who've been behind before so I know just how to help you catch up." Penelope smiled. She was a truly beautiful woman with her rich brunette hair pinned up into a soft bun. Her sweet, oval-shaped face was kind, her hazel eyes friendly. She was petite and willowy and radiated an air of calm grace. Just the sort of lady you would want teaching children. She held out one hand to Bea. "Come, I'll show you and Annie around the classroom. Let's get you assigned to a desk."

"Will I have a desk mate?" Bea asked eagerly, less pale and uncertain as she took her new teacher's hand. "Can it be someone nice?"

"Well, let's see." Penelope led them into the large and modern schoolroom with tidy rows of built-in desks, their wooden tops gleaming in the lamplight. A pot-bellied stove sat in the middle of the room, billowing out heat. The teacher's desk stood in the front, off to one side, and behind it on the front wall was a long span of chalkboards.

"Annie," Bea turned around to whisper, her eyes wide. Hope flickered there, pushing out all her fears and worries.

"I know," Annie whispered back, understanding just what her little sister meant. The schoolroom was so nice, surely it meant it would be a pleasant place to learn and maybe make a friend or two. Annie desperately hoped so, for Bea's sake.

"Clarice Breckenridge is all by herself at this desk here." Penelope stopped in front of a desk not too far from the stove, on the outside aisle near the window. "She's about your age. She's very nice. I think you two will get along well."

"Oh, thank you." Bea stared at her desk, her hopes for friends and a normal life lighting her up, fueling her returning exuberance. "I had to go to school at the orphanage before, and we had to do our work first. We only got lessons after supper and it was one of the workers teaching us. She wasn't a real teacher."

"I'm sure she did her best for you all. I admire her for that," Penelope said gently. The compassion in her eyes made Annie like her more. The teacher offered a smile. "Annie, I'll take good care of your sister, trust me. You are welcome to visit during our lunch hour, many parents and guardians come by to deliver forgotten lunches or just to check on their children. I want you to feel as if you can talk to me about anything. Bea is so important, and I'll do everything I can to help her with her education."

"I'm very grateful for that," Annie said sincerely. "And I'm so glad to meet you."

"That's just how I feel." Penelope smiled, and in that smile Annie saw a friend. "I look forward to getting to know you better. Oh, it sounds like the Dunbar boys have arrived. No one else can make quite that much noise in such a short amount of time."

Annie tilted her head, listening to the stomp of little boy feet, the bang of the door slamming shut, the good-natured argument between them that resulted in a thud—as if a little body had been shoved against a wall.

"I'd best go intervene," Penelope said sweetly, laughter in her eyes. "Bea, please make sure you warm up thoroughly at the stove. I'll be right back."

Penelope marched off, her caramel-colored wool dress swishing around her heels. Annie brushed Bea's bangs, just to touch her, just to fuss with her a little.

"Someone will be here to pick you up after school," Annie promised. "I don't know if it will be me or Cal the stable boy. I haven't talked to Aumaleigh about time off in the afternoon to come get you."

"I'll be okay," Bea said, her gaze drifting over to the entryway, where a quiet girl about Bea's age entered. She had brown braids, a button face and a shy demeanor. Maybe it was Clarice? Annie thought so, since the girl looked at the desk where Bea stood hesitantly and smiled.

Annie gave Bea a quick hug and left. She waved goodbye to Penelope who was busy separating two identical twin boys and biting her lip to keep from laughing at their antics. Light of heart, Annie burst out into the cold, drawing her scarf around her neck. A handful of children were within sight, trudging through the snowy yard or the street near Adam.

Adam. She wished her heart didn't kick when she saw him. He rose from the seat, covering it carefully with the buffalo robe to keep the snow off and tipped his hat in her direction. Tall and steely, he worked to remove Phil's blanket. Phil spotted her and gave a friendly head toss, as if he was glad to see her.

It really did feel like something out of a dream, she thought, as she hopped off the last step and into the snow. A little girl, about waist high, scampered by her, all dressed in pink. When Annie looked up at one of the windows, Bea hadn't come up to the glass to wave goodbye. Maybe that meant she was making friends with Clarice.

Phil gave a snort, as if he was unhappy she was heading straight to the sleigh instead of him. He stomped his foot and swished his tail.

"I think he wants you to greet him properly." Adam chuckled, kneeling down to loosen the buckle at Phil's belly. "You'd be wise to bring him a sugar cube or a carrot. If you do, I think he'll likely wind up being your best friend."

"I could use a best friend," Annie laughed, she just felt so happy. "Even if it's a horse."

"Sometimes there's no better friend than a horse," Adam informed her, keeping his back to her as he folded Phil's blanket. "I have four of them and I spend more time with my horses than with people."

"Sure, because you're on the road so much." Annie watched him stride away to stow the blanket, and gave Phil the nose pat he was expecting. The gelding batted his long black curly eyelashes at her, making it impossible not to fall for him. "I think you and I are going to be great friends, Phil. What do you think?"

Phil lowered his big head for her to rub all the way up to his forehead. What a sweetie. She brushed snow out of his forelock so it wouldn't fall into his eyes. She gave one final glance over her shoulder at the schoolhouse windows, wishing good things for Bea's first day.

"Are you ready?" Adam asked patiently in that mesmerizing way he had. It was as if the timbre of his voice, the rumble and vibration of it, curled around her like a blanket.

Affected, she didn't trust her voice so she nodded. She lifted her skirts and clomped through the deep snow, drawing nearer to him with each step. Her skin tingled. The hair on her arms stood on end. The empty places in her heart opened, like a door swinging wide. He too said nothing as he held the buffalo robe for her and offered her a hand as she climbed onto the seat. Why was she aware of his every movement? Why could she sense each breath he took?

She slid over, putting plenty of space between them as he settled in, big and towering, somehow shrinking that distance with his presence.

He gestured at the reins laying on the dash. Woodenly, she reached for them, adjusted them in her hands as Phil waited, ears back, eager for her command.

"I was thinking we could drive back a different way." She gave the reins a light snap and Phil took off, pulling them along amiably. "I guess I could do it another time, but I'm curious is all. I'd like to see what the houses look like."

"Of course, I remember you talking about wanting a place for you and Bea." He settled against the cushion, the foot or so of space separating them seemed to shrink dangerously. "Sometimes it's good to take a look at what you want so you can dream. That makes it easier to work toward it."

"Exactly." She glanced at him through her lashes, glad he understood. "That's the way I think too. My ma always said dreaming was a sure path to disappointment—"

"But if you don't dream, then you have nothing to work toward and no way of getting it," he finished for her.

"That's what I always said to Ma." She smiled at him sweetly. "Ma said it was just a way for me to justify all my daydreaming. That was when I was younger, when I was different. I had a lot of dreams."

"Life has a way of taking them out of you sometimes," he admitted, thinking of her losses and the people she'd had to say goodbye to—a father, a mother and a newborn, not to mention an older brother who'd abandoned her in Landville (according to rumor). "You must have some dreams left, though."

"Just one." She reined to the right onto the cross street, taking them along a snowy residential lane. Many tracks had packed down the snow, making the going much easier for Phil. Annie sighed, unaware of the dreamy look on her lovely face or the shimmer in her light blue eyes. "I want Bea to have a normal life and a much better one than I had."

"It seems to me you have a good start on that dream." He resisted the urge to drape his arm across her shoulders and draw her close, to warm her with his body heat because she looked cold. Her adorable sloping nose had turned red from the wind and he could see her shivering.

"Without Aumaleigh, we wouldn't be this far. I want to work hard to make it up to her, for giving us a chance." Annie glanced at the street of simple but cozy homes. Some had porches, others big windows, likely far out of a kitchen worker's price range. But still, it didn't hurt to dream. Annie sighed, studying each house as they went by. "If Aumaleigh hadn't answered my letter, I would still be in Landville working two jobs and Bea would be in that orphanage."

"This is a good chance for both of you." His chest hurt thinking about Annie's future here. "You have a secure job, because I don't think your aunt has the heart to fire anyone. You could have your own home someday. There's no reason why you won't find a lot of happiness here. Maybe you'll marry someone?"

Surely suitors would come calling, he reasoned. Perhaps one would be a good and decent man who would treat her well. Imagining her happily married to another man nearly killed him, but he forced a smile, forced himself to think not of his pain but of her happiness.

"A job and a place to live are all I need," she said simply, glancing down the side street as they headed up the next block. "I don't have the heart left for another marriage, not that my vows to Harold were ever really real. It is too much to trust another man, any man, with my life and with Bea's. When Harold brought me home from the church, I thought he was going to be such a wonderful husband. He'd just swept me off my feet."

"Well, sure," he said tightly, remembering the salesman who'd come to town, who was friend to all. "That's why you married him."

"But he changed the instant the ceremony ended," she confessed, her voice hardly more than a thin whisper. "He sent me walking uptown to get groceries for supper, he demanded I do it, showing his temper. I should have argued right then, I should have done anything but go. He took Bea away after I left for the store. I came back and they were gone. He put her in that orphanage, and by the time I learned the truth I couldn't do anything. He told them I was not to take her out. He was my legal husband, or so I thought, so he had the law on his side. He was in charge of me and Bea. I was forbidden to even see her."

"That had to have broken your heart." It certainly broke his. "It would be hard to trust any man after that."

"Exactly. This way no one could try and separate us." She drew Phil to a stop in the middle of the vacant road. Windows up and down the block glowed with lamplight and the air smelled pleasantly of the wood smoke rising up in gray plumes from so many chimneys. She sighed wistfully. "The houses are smaller here, just shanties. This might be a good street to dream on."

"There's a little cottage for sale on the corner." He pointed to it, a plain square box of a house looking lonely with its dark windows. It looked to be just a few rooms, but it looked enormous compared to the shanty next door. It was painted a buttery yellow and the covered porch gave it a smiling look. If she loved him, Adam thought, he would buy it for her. Longing filled him, longing for what could not be. He cleared his throat. "You and Bea would look good in that house, don't you think?"

"How could we not?" She smiled, a real smile, bright and dazzling. She snapped Phil's reins and the gelding lunged forward obligingly. "What about you? What do you dream of, Adam?"

"Me? I've only had one dream," he confessed, and he was looking at her. "But it was out of my reach."

"I've had many of those dreams." Sympathy and understanding crinkled in the corners of her eyes, rang tenderly in her voice. "Somehow you just have to keep going without them and hope that a better dream is out there somewhere waiting to find you. Getting Bea back was that dream for me. There has to be one for you too. That's what I want for you, Adam."

"Like I said, I've only had the one dream, the woman I loved, and it passed me by." Muscles bunched along his jaw, as he leaned in, his eyes dark and deep enough to fall into. "She didn't love me and right now, I don't want any other dream."

"Oh." She didn't know what to say to that, likely because her brain wasn't working properly. Maybe it had something to do with how near he was, closing in, until his Stetson's brim shielded her from the falling snow.

He reached with one large hand to tug up her scarf. She felt the knit yarn stretch and tighten, and watched the clouds of her breath and his merge as he deftly straightened the fabric around her neck. His irises had gone black, and there was something infinitely tender there, in those dark depths. Her breath stalled and her heart forgot to beat as she sat there, as if paralyzed. The entire world faded away. There were only the two of them, just her and Adam, and the feathered brush of his leather glove against her cheek as he wrapped her scarf for her, covering her mouth and nose.

"So you don't get cold," he said, his baritone pleasant, such a wonderful sound.

Such a wonderful man, she thought, her heart fluttering. "Thank you."

"Sure, since your hands were busy with the reins," he explained. A grin hooked one side of his mouth, hinting at dimples as he tucked the buffalo robe snugly around her, making sure no icy wind could gust in.

It was nice, this feeling of being taken care of by him. Maybe it was the best feeling she'd ever known.

"Good thing Phil knows his way." Adam gave a soft bark of laughter, sitting back against the cushions. "You're a good man, Phil."

Phil arched his neck at that and gave his mane a proud toss. This was not news to him. Phil led them along the final block of town and into the open countryside heading home. The road was a little more beaten down and easier for the gelding to plod along. As they passed the untouched stretch of what had been the road to Deer Springs to her right, Annie was very thankful indeed that Adam had decided to stay until the conditions improved.

It was hard to tell if it was only concern for an easier journey for him, or if it was because she didn't want him to leave. She turned her attention to the road ahead, but she could not ignore the man at her side, the man who made her feel things she never had before.

CHAPTER TEN

Throughout the day, random thoughts of Adam plagued her. Annie dunked her hands into the wash water, coming up with the measuring spoon she'd been short when she'd dried the set earlier. Her gaze went straight to the window, where the snow fell lighter now and not as gusty. This morning, when they'd returned from town, Adam had left her at the back door and drove Phil into the barn to rub him down. Not long after, Adam left with a group of the hired men going up into the hills hunting for wild turkey. Thanksgiving was tomorrow.

"I think we have enough pie to satisfy the hungry horde," Josslyn declared good-naturedly as she put the last pumpkin pie in the oven. "Those cowboys can eat pie faster than you've ever seen. Annie, having you here was a big help. The baking went much faster. Louisa, you have a gift for pie making. Even I can't get the pie dough that flaky. Now, on to the bread."

"It's still rising," Louisa called out, checking beneath the cloths covering the two big bowls of bread dough near the stove. "It will be a while yet."

"Then you girls take a well-earned break." Josslyn closed the oven door carefully. "Go on, off with you both. I don't want to see you back here until I call."

"Oh, I'm going to work on my knitting." Louisa blew a tendril of brown hair out of her eyes, flushed with pleasure. "It's a Christmas gift for my sister, and I keep worrying I won't get it done in time."

"Then you go knit," Josslyn encouraged as she poured herself a cup of tea. "I want to hear those needles clacking."

"Thanks, Josslyn." Louisa hurried into the small bedroom off the kitchen, her skirts rustling.

"And I'll be upstairs," Annie told her boss, wishing she could keep her mind focused, but it kept boomeranging right back to Adam and the morning's sleigh ride. He was such a big, rugged man, but his capacity for tenderness captivated her. She simply couldn't forget it.

"I imagine you have more unpacking to do," Josslyn said as she reached for the sugar bowl. "It always takes a while to get settled. That's why I vowed never to move again. I have a little house on Alpine Lane and it's just right for me. I tell everyone that's why I can't get married, no one else would fit in that shanty."

"Oh, I drove up Alpine Lane this morning." Annie spun around, halfway to the stairs. "I love the trees lining the street. It looks like a nice place to live."

"I'm happy there." Josslyn smiled, rolling her eyes toward the ceiling when someone knocked on the door. "Wouldn't you know it? The instant I decide to take a break. No, you go on upstairs, I'll deal with whoever it is. Let's hope it's not the men back with the turkeys. They'll drag in snow and dirt and dead turkeys."

Annie couldn't help laughing as she headed up the steps. The sound of the door opening echoed through the kitchen and a man's deep voice she didn't recognize greeted Josslyn cordially. It sounded like ranch business, so Annie retreated to her room. Yes, she thought looking around, she really needed to get this place settled.

Crates were stacked in one corner, just waiting to be emptied so she knelt down in front of them. There, in the top one, sat a folded quilt. She ran her fingertips over the scalloped edging. Ma had told many stories of her and Grandma sewing this together one long winter, when grandfather had gone south to find work. Alone, the females in the family had run the farm, which had been devastated by drought the summer before, and pinched pennies trying to make ends meet. The quilt had been pieced with cloth cut from out-grown and worn-out dresses.

Annie's chest went tight with the memories. She ran her thumb across a yellow gingham patchwork square, made from Ma's favorite dress when she'd been six. Ma had worn the dress on her first day of school, the story went. Annie sighed, almost feeling her ma in the room—her gentleness, her love.

I've lived without love for so long, Annie thought, placing a hand over her heart. It was almost as if her heart had died, not just merely broken. When Harold had shown his true self and turned into a heavy drinker, like her pa, it had cut deep, leaving scars in her heart she'd never recovered from. Her naive dreams of happily-ever-after perished in the wake of brutal reality (she'd been married two weeks before her eighteenth birthday).

Those five months of marriage had been the most hopeless in her young life. Harold had made her work, he'd taken her paycheck as if he'd earned it and made her pawn everything she had of value— including her mother's only piece of jewelry. He'd watched her so closely she had no chance of running away and stealing Bea from the orphanage on the way out of town. Because of those hard months of fear and being treated as worthless, she had come to understand her mother's life too well.

It was a pattern Bea would not repeat, Annie vowed. She'd give her life to keep it from happening. She stood, shaking out the quilt, the first quilt her mother had pieced. She held it tightly, as if to soak up that long ago love, as if it would comfort her from the upset of what she had felt for Adam earlier today. Because she'd been aware of him—and attracted. She'd wanted something she could not possibly have.

She heard the back door open and more male voices rang through the house. The hunters had returned and Adam with them. She couldn't hear his voice in the cacophony of men down below, but she could feel his presence, as if a ribbon tied her heart to his. Her feelings for him were like a lamp burning, growing ever stronger.

Tears stood in her eyes as she spread the quilt over the top of the double mattress, folding it carefully. No matter how good the man, she did not want to love—she *would* not love—not ever again.

* * *

Adam was used to snowstorms waylaying him on the road, but as he looked around the barn in the late afternoon, he'd never had a more pleasant layover anywhere. Annie's aunt had gone out of her way to make it clear he was welcome to stay for as long as he wanted, and the cowboys were a friendly bunch. Their trek into the hills (they hadn't gone far, not in that deep snow) had been more fun than anything, full of joking and laughter. They'd caught five wild turkeys (big ones, too). After dressing them and handing them over to Josslyn in the kitchen, the men had retreated to the bunkhouse for another round of poker.

But Adam wasn't much of a gambling man, and he liked to use his time productively. He'd spent the last half of the afternoon in the back of the barn, where the men had a workshop for working wood and leather. While he sorted through scrap lumber, pieced and nailed and sanded, his mind kept drifting to Annie over there in the kitchen house helping with the holiday cooking. Not long ago Cal had fetched the girls from school and dropped Bea off at the house. She looked happy as she'd danced across the back porch. That meant Annie would be happy, too. He was glad things were working out well for her.

And he was glad he'd spent time with her alone this morning. For a moment, when he'd been adjusting her scarf, he'd thought he saw something like awareness in her eyes. But she'd been very clear about not wanting to marry. *I don't have the heart left for another marriage,* she'd said. She'd sounded pretty clear about that. He didn't doubt her, and that meant he had no chance with her. Still, that wouldn't stop him from doing things for her. Determined, he bowed his head, walking to the end of the aisle.

"Enjoying your time off, boys?" he asked his team who were lodged in roomy box stalls near the front of the barn. Buddy opened one eye and closed it again, going back to his drowsing. Dusty pushed against his gate, eager for a nose pet so Adam obliged, giving him a good rub. In the neighboring stall, Jasper stretched his neck over his gate, brown eyes begging for the same treatment. Rocky lifted his head, ears pricked, his gaze fastened on something he could see down the hill.

Adam looked, too. The kitchen door had swung open and a slender, willowy blond rushed out. Annie. She had covered her head and shoulders with a big, wool shawl. Even from so far away, he could see the change in her, catching glimpses of the young woman she used to be when he'd first fallen in love with her. There was a bounce to her step as she rang the dinner bell. She looked relaxed and settled. She was happy, and that was what mattered. She glanced up and spotted him in the barn door watching her. She lifted a hand and smiled.

His heart brimmed. He tipped his hat in her direction, watching as she swirled away, retreating back into the kitchen. He stood there with his heart spellbound. He laid his hand over his coat pocket and felt the gift he'd been carrying around for her, tucked there since he'd left Wyoming, a token of his devotion to her. He remembered that sad summer day when he'd caught sight of her walking in her patched blue calico, head down, her face hidden by her fraying sunbonnet brim, hurrying down the street visible from the alley.

That day he'd been unloading grain bags he'd fetched from the train depot. Sweat poured down the back of his neck, dampening his shirt as he'd hefted one hundred and fifty pound bags onto his shoulder and carried them into the back of the feed store. The jeweler next door came over, shaking his head.

"That was the saddest thing I've seen in a long time." Mr. Dolan wiped his glasses on his shirt. "That young lady came to sell her dead mother's locket. You could tell it broke her heart to part with it, but her husband made her do it."

"Don't know what's wrong with some men these days." Grim, Mr. Sims, the feed store owner, raked a hand through his thinning gray hair. "Men weren't like that in my day."

Twenty minutes later, Adam had plunked down the last grain bag, tipped his hat to Mr. Sims and headed straight to the jewelry store. He asked for that locket and bought it. He couldn't stand the thought of a stranger buying it. He'd had it all these years, not knowing how to give it to her. What did he say? *I've been secretly in love with you, even though I'm a stranger to you, and bought your mother's locket.* No, he thought, taking his hand off his pocket. He would have sounded like a mad man, an idiot or a stalker. Either way, she wouldn't have been impressed.

But it was time to return it. His plan was to do it before he left, which would be after she rejected him, after she'd broken his heart for good. But that wouldn't stop him from loving her.

No, nothing on this earth could do that.

The snow stopped falling and a hazy sun peeked through the clouds, casting weak, long shadows as he headed down the hill. He joined the other men filing into the kitchen, taking off their wraps and kicking off their boots, some joking with Josslyn on their way to the table. Annie was busy at the stove ladling gravy into a bowl, and didn't look up when he passed. He suspected she knew he was there, with his gaze glued to her.

Yeah, he thought, resigned. His plan sounded just about right.

* * *

"I knew I had one!" Aumaleigh sounded victorious as she backed out of the storage room at the end of the hall. The lamplight found her, gleaming darkly in her molasses colored hair and polishing her porcelain complexion. She handed Bea the school slate. "It's not new, but it's serviceable. It's the one I had when I went to school."

"I'll be extra special careful with it," Bea promised, clutching the slate to her chest. "I'm so grateful on account of now I can practice my spelling and arithmetic at my desk and not on the blackboard between everyone else's lessons. Thank you so, so much, Aumaleigh."

"Yes, thank you, Aumaleigh." Annie closed the storage door for their aunt. "We'll get it back to you as soon as possible."

"Oh, no need. It's not like I was using it anyway, and it was just going to waste sitting there gathering dust." Aumaleigh waved away any concern with a sweep of her slender hand. "You just keep it, Bea. I'm glad it'll be getting some use. I just wish I had kept my old schoolbooks. They would come in handy about now."

"That's okay," Bea said over her shoulder as she skipped down the hallway. "Teacher is letting me use her books for now. She had an extra set."

"Which is very nice of her." Another reason to like Penelope, Annie thought as she followed Bea down the stairs to the kitchen. Bea pulled out a chair at the round oak table and hunkered down to practice her spelling. The kitchen was empty, with supper over and the dishes done. Light crept beneath Louisa's closed bedroom door, otherwise the house was dark.

"Are you sure you don't want an advance on your wages?" Aumaleigh lifted her coat from a wall hook and slipped into it. "You would be able to buy Bea's books that way."

"Thank you, but I'd rather earn the wages first." Although she was touched by the offer, she didn't want to take advantage of her aunt. "Besides, Bea's teacher says that's why she keeps an extra set to lend out. It's not a trouble to anyone that the books are being borrowed."

"All right, but I worry about you girls." Aumaleigh buttoned up and reached for her scarf. "If there's anything you need before payday, you let me know."

Annie nodded in agreement, earning Aumaleigh's gentle smile. She was used to earning her own way, but it was nice to have someone to lean on, if they should need it. It meant more than she could say.

"Remember, you and Bea are invited to Thanksgiving dinner with your cousins." Aumaleigh pulled a knit hat out of her pocket and pulled it on. "Josslyn will be in bright and early to get the turkeys in the oven. We'll get the meal on the table here at noon for the men and then you, Bea and me will walk up to spend the rest of the day with the girls. It will be great fun, so sleep well and I'll see you first thing."

Aumaleigh opened the door and disappeared into the night. Moonshine spilled across the landscape, shining almost purple on the dark expanse of snow. Annie sighed, content, and closed the door.

"That was really nice of Aumaleigh," Bea commented, slate pencil scratching. Her big blue eyes shone with emotion. "Who knew through all that sad time when we were in Wyoming, that we would end up here? It's better than what I could have dreamed up."

"That's how I feel too." Gratitude was a small word to describe it. Annie shivered. "Brr, it's getting cold. I'd better put more wood on the fire. Do you have enough light to see by? I can bring over another lamp."

"I can see just fine." Bea bent over her work, book open next to her, Aumaleigh's slate in front of her. She looked happy, like a girl was supposed to be. "Clarice was nice and let me practice some on her slate today. We ate lunch together."

"I'm glad you've made a friend." Annie hoped there would be more friends for Bea in the future, lots of fun times and more wishes coming true. She opened the stove door and tossed in a few sticks of wood. "It's too bad you don't have school tomorrow."

"I know, because I can't wait to go back." Bea's slate pencil scratched away. "When Cal picked me up, he said he'd just drive me too. He takes Hailie to school now anyway."

"Do I know who Hailie is?" Annie asked, closing the door.

"It's Mr. Beckett's little girl," Bea explained, turning the page in her spelling book. "He's the ranch foreman, you know."

"Yes, I've heard something like that." Annie tousled Bea's hair on the way by, standing some of her blond bangs up on end. "You study, I'm going upstairs to mend a few of your socks."

She left Bea in the kitchen and had one foot on the bottom step when the back door opened a man's shadow moved into the entry way. She recognized that shadow—tall, mighty and composed. Adam.

"Annie?" His familiar baritone echoed against the walls. He emerged from the darkness and seeing him, her breath caught in her lungs, her ribs cinched tight. The memory of his touch against her as he'd drawn up her scarf today made her shiver.

"It must be cold out there." She wrapped her arms around her chest, as if to create a barrier between them so he wouldn't affect her so much. "Would you like something warm to drink? I could steep some tea or make coffee."

"No, you've had a long workday. I'm fine." He shook his head, scattering his thick mane of black hair. A five o'clock shadow clung to his jaw line. His masculine presence seemed to chase away every last bit of oxygen as he towered over her. He set something box-like he carried on the nearby bench and shrugged out of his coat. "It's stopped snowing out there."

"Finally." She felt self-conscious, aware of her faded work dress and the patch on her sleeve. "You must be eager to get going."

"Not eager." He shook his head once. Pleasant, manly crinkles cut into the skin around his eyes. "I've heard word that the roads are improving, so I'll head out soon enough. How is the unpacking going?"

"It's done," she managed to answer in a wheezing-like way. It seemed that her arms shielding her chest was ineffective against him, and that was something she did not want to think about too much. "We're all settled in."

"Good. I was thinking I could haul out the crates and boxes for you, and see if there's room in the corner for the rocking chair to fit."

"That would be nice of you." It really was. She took a step back, studying the man. Blue flannel stretched across his muscled shoulders and chest, bringing out the dark flecks in his eyes. Denims hugged his hips and long legs. He was a powerful man, no doubt about that, but he had a great capacity for kindness. Was that what she found so attractive? Was that why she couldn't stop her heart from leaning toward him, like a summer flower to the sun?

"Although I'm not sure if the chair will fit," she continued in a shaky voice, unhappy with her reaction to him. Why couldn't she control her feelings? She shuffled forward, leading him across the kitchen. "I'd hate to have you haul the chair all the way over only to have to take it back."

"I'll measure first." He strode after her, a wooden box tucked under one arm. She didn't take the time to study it, because she was trying not to look in his direction. She bypassed Bea, who glanced up from her borrowed slate and book to watch curiously. As she climbed up the stairs, she felt the comfort of his presence behind her every step of the way.

CHAPTER ELEVEN

"I made this for you." Adam set the wooden box on the bureau, hovering in the doorway as if too much of a gentleman to invite himself in all the way.

"For me?" she asked with surprise, studying the honey-gold wood, carefully sanded and pieced together. It was much larger than a jewelry box, but it looked very much like one, with a hinged top. When she looked closer, two hearts were carved into the lid entwined, beneath some lettering. Curious, she leaned closer to read it. But it was a name, one she recognized. *Ginny.* Like a punch, she reeled back, tears stinging her eyes.

"Back in Landville, when I was loading up your things out of that shed," he explained, gently, in hushed tones. "I happened to see the crate with the things you'd made for your baby. I thought a crate isn't a place to keep something special like that."

"Oh." Shocked, she rocked back on her heels, touched by his thoughtfulness. He understood her loss and her love for her little girl—that great, infinite, bright, bright love. Her hands shook as she wiped her eyes. "Adam, I can't believe you made this. I mean, it had to have taken you a long time. You should have been relaxing in the bunkhouse."

"I like to stay busy." He shrugged one brawny shoulder, a casual gesture, like this was no big deal. "I don't mind a game of cards now and then, but it's not how I like to spend my free time. I wanted to do something that mattered."

"I see," she said quietly, overwhelmed. Look what he'd done, the hours this must have taken, not to mention the skill. She lifted the lid. Inside was a carefully sanded interior, deep enough to hold Ginny's things. "I don't know what to say. There are no words."

"Well, I'm glad you like it." He moved past her, so close her entire body shivered—including her soul.

"All the crates are empty, I see," he said in his honest, get-it-done kind of way, as if he hadn't just touched her heart. He studied her with the same intensity she'd felt earlier today in the sleigh.

He really cares for me, she thought, hand to her throat. He hadn't made the box because he had time on his hands. It was a gift.

"I'll get these out of your way." He interrupted her thoughts, hefting up the crates and boxes easily. "Why don't you fill up that box?"

"Okay." She reached for the bureau's bottom drawer, trying so hard to hold her feelings in. Because whatever they were or however strong they were becoming, she could not act on them. She did care for Adam. Very, very much.

The dream of real, happily-ever-after love for her was gone forever. She'd learned to be a practical woman. Harold had taught her a valuable lesson, one she would never forget. When you married a man, you were placing your life in his hands—and all those you loved. And not just Bea, she thought, tears gathering in a lump in her throat.

She'd trusted Ginny with a man who'd abandoned her, who hadn't cared enough to stay for her birth, much less hold her lovingly in his arms as she gasped her last breath. Annie's eyes burned. Oh, how she hurt with love and grief, remembering.

As she listened to Adam in the hallway, setting down his armload with a clatter of wood, she tugged open the bottom bureau drawer. She lifted the impossibly small things she'd knitted—socks, booties, sweaters out of yarn Jo Ellen had given her. She laid the little clothes out on the bureau top, the love she'd put into every stitch filling her once again.

"There's not enough room for the rocking chair," Adam said, leaning against the doorframe. "I'll tarp the chair up really good, so it will be protected there in the carriage house."

"Okay, thanks." Her voice sounded croaky and when she cleared it, that lump stuck in her throat refused to budge. "We can get by without the chair."

"When you rent that shanty one day, you'll have room for it there." Adam radiated that patient, unwavering presence of his. Her heart fluttered with longing that was far more than physical attraction.

"Is there anything I can do for you?" he asked patiently.

"You've done so much already," she told him, hearing her feelings for him revealed in her voice. "You've gone way beyond the call of duty. I still don't know how to thank you."

"Thanks isn't necessary." He pushed away from the door and stalked closer, his steps slow, his presence powerful. Annie shivered all the way to her soul.

"It was my pleasure to help out." He towered over her, standing between her and the lamplight. "If you need anything, ever, you just ask."

"I'll keep that in mind." She couldn't explain the urge to reach out to him, a need she had to fight. She backed into the bureau, feeling dizzy and breathless and afraid to examine why. He did this to her. She cleared her throat, trying to keep her feelings from her voice. "When are you leaving?"

"In the morning, if the clear weather holds." The lamplight caught on one side of his face, shining on the angled cut of his high cheekbone and on the whisker stubble dark on his jaw.

Her fingers itched to reach out and touch him there, to know the feel and texture of his whiskers. She gripped the top of the bureau instead. "Tomorrow is Thanksgiving. You would travel on a holiday?"

"I have no reason to stay, unless—" His blue gaze turned dark, full of intensity and kindness. Caring shone in those depths, the kind of brightness she used to dream about. He hesitated, as if gathering his thoughts or his courage. "I hope you've had a chance to get to know me and that you wouldn't mind if I came courting."

"Courting?" She repeated the word, ignoring the thrill in her chest, that strange, wild rising of hope. For one brief moment, she let herself imagine she might say yes, let herself picture what it would be like to have Adam come courting. He'd pick her up, take her hand to help her into the seat. He could take her driving and always be the perfect gentlemen. His thoughtful and kind nature would show in every word and every deed.

But she knew better. Fairy tale love didn't happen to a girl like her.

She'd stopped believing it could.

"No, I'm sorry." She felt her heart break as she said those words. She wished she could be that girl she'd once been, who believed in true love that endured no matter what. But she was no longer that girl. She'd learned the hard way that no one—not even a man as wonderful as Adam—was going to love her like that. No man could. "I really am not looking for another husband. I have Bea to think about."

"Of course you do." His answer was steady, laden with understanding, because that's who he was. His throat worked as if he'd taken a hard blow. But his shoulders stayed strong. He was a strong man. "I knew that's what you were going to say, but I had to ask."

"Oh, Adam." She couldn't help laying her hand on his chest because she wanted to feel the reliable beat of his heart, to feel connected to him for a few moments longer. Saying no to him was breaking her heart. "I'm so sorry."

"Me, too." He nodded once, meeting her gaze. Pain glistened in his eyes, honest and unguarded. He'd put everything on the line and she'd hurt him.

It surprised her to see how much. Her jaw went slack as he walked away, back straight, muscles bunched, a powerful man trying not to show his wounds. He disappeared through the doorway, from her sight. The crates clattered as he lifted them. His boots struck the stairs as he made his way to the kitchen. Her heart broke all over again.

She'd seen the pain in his eyes. A sob caught in her throat. Agonized, she realized just how much she'd hurt him. It didn't make sense. How could she mean that much to him? They'd only just gotten to know each other. She sat down on the edge of the bed, listening to the last knell of his footsteps downstairs and the back door clicking shut. He was gone, and he'd taken her heart with him. Her broken, disbelieving heart.

* * *

Her rejection was exactly what he'd expected, Adam thought as he shut the carriage house doors and stepped into the night. He was really hurt. Annie had gently and kindly shattered him, and he was never going to recover. That's how deeply he felt for her.

He breathed deep, drawing frigid air into his lungs, letting the shock burn away every other feeling in his chest—but it didn't work. Nothing could ever drown out this agony. Annie would never be his. He squared his shoulders, resolved to do his best to accept it. The icy surface of the snow crackled beneath his boots as he cut across the hill.

That's where he'd gone sledding with her. He could still hear the music of her laughter in the air, the joy on her dear face, the way her blue eyes glittered. She was happy here, and that knowledge was his only silver lining as he trudged along.

Moonlight shone across the snow, opalescent; a deep, dark purple glow. The inky sky overhead flickered with thousands of stars. Those stunning points of light glinted in colors—white, yellow, red, blue—so brightly it felt like a sign. That for as long as Annie lived here with her aunt, everything was going to be all right for her. *That* mattered to him. All he wanted was her happiness.

Still, he felt sorely alone as he cut across the hill. He had no future. His heart was shattered. He would never forget the true regret on her face, poignant in her eyes, when she'd turned him down. At least he knew she cared about him—just not enough.

But for a moment, they had been close. For a little while, he got to spend time with her. She had just filled his heart.

But he had his answer, and it was time to move on. His heart felt as frosty as the night, frozen still, unable to feel. It was best to keep it that way.

He stepped into the light from the bunkhouse windows, opened the door and stepped into the warmth.

"Adam!" Kellan looked up from his side of a chess board, a black pawn in hand. "We were wondering where you were. We almost sent out a search party to find you."

"I had just a few last minute things to do," he explained, pulling off his gloves. "The storm is over and there isn't a cloud in sight. I'll be gone at first light. It's a long drive home."

With any luck, he'd be gone before Annie was in the kitchen. He didn't think his heart could take seeing her again.

"I can't blame you there," Burton spoke up, shuffling cards at the table. His gaze held sympathy, as if he'd been wise to Adam's feelings all along. "Just know you're always welcome here. Anytime."

"I appreciate that." Adam slung his hat onto a wall peg. He crossed the room, his gloves still clutched in one hand. He went to shove them into his coat pocket and realized something was already in there.

Annie's locket. He rolled his eyes, frustrated with himself. He'd forgotten to give it to her. An arrow of pain speared deep into his frozen heart as he ambled down the hallway. The wound in his heart hurt, and it was going to hurt for a long time. He let out a slow sigh. He loved her and nothing, not even her rejection, was going to change it.

* * *

The moon had slipped away from her bedroom window, no longer tossing platinum around the edges of the curtain. Annie shifted onto her side, the bed ropes creaking beneath her. She waited, wondering if the noise would wake Bea. But, no, her little sister slept on, sprawled on her stomach on the other side of the bed, her nightcap askew.

I wish I could sleep that easily, Annie thought wryly as she snuggled into her pillow. She didn't know how many hours had slipped by, but she knew the reason why she was still awake. Adam. He'd wanted to court her. Tears prickled behind her eyes, which wasn't helping her quest for sleep.

The box he'd made her showed thoughtfulness she still couldn't process or accept. Men didn't treat her that way. There was her father—a man who was a drunk, unable to keep a steady job, whose irresponsibility was the reason she'd grown up in extreme poverty. His friends had leered at her; she was marked by her father's reputation. In a small town, children were often judged by their parents' behavior.

When she'd been old enough to marry, she'd been working to support her mother and siblings, not attending social events with friends. The men she had contact with were mostly those she worked with—and they hadn't always been the decent kind, not at the hotel where she cleaned, especially. Then her mother had died, and there had been no chance for a nice beau—not after her brother left her alone to raise Bea.

And then Harold had come along and treated her like a lady. She thought he had been able to look past her patched, handed-down calico dresses to the real girl she was inside. He'd certainly acted that way. He was like a shining knight, the one truly marvelous thing that ever happened to her.

But it had all been a lie, she remembered, pain throbbing in her chest, as if from an old, bleeding wound. He'd just been pretending. He hadn't seen any value in her at all except for what he could get out of her. She had to keep her jobs, she had to watch him spend her money and without any legal right to stop him. He scared her, he criticized her and he even hit her. When his real wife's father tracked him down, Harold took every last penny she had, sold her dishes and the cookstove and escaped before the wife's father could haul him back to Colorado.

When word spread around town about how her marriage to Harold had never been legal, that made her little more than a kept woman. She'd learned to walk down the boardwalks in town with her eyes down, ignoring comments from men and discouraging any kind of sexual interest. But no man could really love her, not after that. She was a shamed woman, she'd lain with a man she wasn't legally married to and bore his child. No man would see her the same after that. No man was going to love her the way she longed to be loved.

Not even Adam. Her heart filled with love for him and she swiped her eyes, hating the weakness of her tears. What she wanted so desperately—to truly be loved by a good, good man—was never going to happen. She had to accept it. She couldn't be tempted to get out of bed and go knocking at Adam's window. Because she did want to say yes to him.

She wished she still believed in true love, the kind that could never be broken, in a love that overthrew life, that was the only thing that mattered. But no one, not even Adam, could love her like that.

So for her sake, and Bea's, she had to do the right thing and let him go.

CHAPTER TWELVE

Aumaleigh reined in her dear mare, Buttons, in front of the ranch's main barn. The doors were open, giving a clear view of Adam Butler, who was leading one of his striking bay draft horses from a stall. What a good man, she thought, watching the way he handled the animal, speaking low to it. But he was clearly leaving. So much for her hopes for him and Annie.

Anyone with eyes could see the young man was smitten. Aumaleigh climbed out of the sleigh, sweeping her wrapped wedding dress from the seat. She wanted to take it to Verbena in a bit, so the girl could take a good look at it and decide for sure if it was what she wanted to wear for her wedding. It was heartening to think of the dress she'd lovingly stitched being worn by her beloved niece. Maybe those dreams of love sewn into it would bring Verbena and Zane the best possible happiness.

She wanted that for all her nieces—including Annie. Maybe that's why she made it her business to mosey on over to see what Adam was up to.

"Sorry!" the stable boy called out, dashing down the aisle. "I'll get Buttons for you."

"Thanks, Cal," Aumaleigh called out as she hurried along, smoothing the dress slung over her arm. Whew, it was bitter this morning. She couldn't stop shivering. It wasn't the best morning for travel.

"Hello, Aumaleigh." Adam was in the middle of backing his horse into the empty traces. The big gelding went obediently, his brown eyes trusting. Adam had that strong, masculine thing going for him—he seemed like a man who could calmly take care of any problem or right any wrong. Just the right kind of young man for dear, dear Annie. Why didn't he seem to know it?

"Good morning, Adam." She came to a stop in the wide aisle of the barn. His wagon box was mounted on sled runners, ready for a long journey on winter roads. His three other horses stood watching from their stalls, as calm and steady as their master. "I didn't know you would be leaving us today."

"I decided last night," he said succinctly, not unfriendly, but not in his usual way either. Clearly something was wrong.

"You do know that it's Thanksgiving," she pointed out, wondering if she could get him to stay. "You shouldn't spend it on the road all alone. Why don't you celebrate with us? I'm sure my nieces would be glad to have you."

"Thank you, but no." He squared his shoulders, a man resolved, before kneeling down to buckle the horse into his rigging. "I need to be on my way."

"I see." She knew the look of a man not about to change his mind, and that saddened her. "I hope when you're in this part of the country, you will come by and see us. I think Annie might like that."

"That's where you're wrong, ma'am." His voice boomed with certainty. He turned around, his work done, and in his kind blue eyes she saw so much pain, she nearly gasped. Something had indeed happened. Something had gone very wrong. He tipped his hat, perhaps to hide that pain from her sight, and cleared his throat. "I can't thank you enough for your hospitality. It's been a pleasure to know you. Good luck to you, ma'am."

"And to you too, Adam." She meant that. He reminded her in a lot of ways of her Gabriel—dependable to a fault, quiet and somewhat shy, but very strong of heart. "Thank you for bringing my nieces safely to me."

"I just gave them a ride from the stage." He shrugged, opening a stall door. "Annie hired me to haul her things, that was all."

That was not all and Aumaleigh knew it, but she sensed how difficult this was for him. She did not want to make it any harder. She knew exactly how a broken heart felt—one broken all the way to the quick.

"Could I ask you to do one thing?" Adam led the next horse over to the traces and left the animal standing. He reached into his pocket and held out a small velvet bag with a jeweler's name sewn onto it in white thread. "This is something that belongs to Annie. Could you give it to her for me?"

"Certainly." When she reached out for it, she saw again the clear and deep grief in his eyes. Poor Adam, she thought, wishing she knew what had happened. Wishing she knew how to fix it.

With a tip of his Stetson, he turned away, intent on his work. She headed across the snowy yard, her steps heavy, wondering what she would find when she walked into the kitchen house. Would Annie have that same shattered look in her eyes?

The hint of the rising sun trailed her, casting a golden-purple blend of light onto the surface of the snow. When she drew near, she caught sight of a face in the window. Annie, with dark shadows beneath her eyes.

The poor girl. In sympathy, instant pain shot through her. Maybe because of the wedding dress she held and the man long ago who hadn't loved her enough to stay.

Love once gone, was gone forever, this Aumaleigh knew for a fact. She thought of that sweet May day when Gabriel had first come calling, and their companionable walk around the lakeshore. He'd picked wild roses for her, he'd brought a basket so they had a picnic of sorts (lemonade and cookies) sitting amid the wildflowers, talking and laughing. She'd never felt such an instant accord with anyone.

And never had again, nearly thirty years later. She did not want that outcome for Annie.

Heart aching, she let herself into the entryway, closed the door behind her and hung the wedding dress on the nearest peg.

"Annie?" she called out, clutching the jeweler's bag. "Could you come here for a moment?"

"Sure," the girl answered in her gentle way, hurrying over, eager to please. The wall sconce tossed lamplight over her as she skidded to a stop. She looked a mess with those big dark circles beneath her eyes, her skin as pale as a sheet. Worse was the haunted sadness clinging to her like a shadow. Whatever happened, it had been terribly painful for them both.

"I ran into Adam at the barn," she said gently, holding up the velvet bag. "He asked me to give this to you."

"A gift?" Distress furrowed across her porcelain forehead, crinkling up her china doll face. "Oh, no, I can't accept another gift from him. That just wouldn't be right."

"I see." Aumaleigh bit her bottom lip. "Adam said that it belongs to you. I assumed it was something of yours he found in his wagon bed."

"No, I've never seen that before." Annie took the little bag, turning it over, studying the jeweler's name. "I don't—"

Then recognition hit and she tugged open the strings holding the bag closed. Her fingers shook and she couldn't hold them steady. Blinking hard to clear her vision, she worked at the little silken strings. The stubborn fabric parted and she reached inside. She felt the familiar fold of paper money. When she pulled it out, it was the thirty-two dollars she'd given Adam to pay for hauling her things. Tucked in with the bills was a small note.

Dear Annie,

I can't accept your money. I never intended to keep it. Money wasn't the reason I took this job. It was never a job to me. There's something else I meant to give you. I was outside the day you sold this. I saw you leaving, but you didn't see me. I know this was your mother's—

Oh, Adam, she thought, too overwhelmed to keep reading. She eagerly upended the bag. A small gold locket on a chain slipped into her hand. Seeing the familiar glint of gold, the engraved roses on the front, a sob broke through her. Her mother's locket, that had been handed down for three generations.

Overcome, Annie squeezed her eyes shut, seeing once again in memory Ma quietly seated on the edge of the bed in their shanty, prying open the locket. Annie had been twelve years old, rushing over from putting away the lunch dishes, eager to gaze at the images inside one more time.

"Are there pictures inside?" Aumaleigh asked in her mellow, caring way.

"Yes." Annie opened her eyes, feeling as if her chest was cracking apart. She'd never thought she would see this locket again. She moved over so Aumaleigh could see too, and shifted the locket, searching for the little lever to open it. Then a terrible thought occurred to her—what if the images were gone? Heart pounding, palms sweating, she opened the locket and there they were—Grandma's smile wreathing her entire face, her arms around Ma on her wedding day. And the other side, cut in the heart-shape of the locket was the second image, just as dear—Ma, Bea and her, standing together.

Annie's gaze savored her mother's sweet smile—oh, it was so good to see. Overcome, deeply grateful, she drank in the sight of Ma's curly ringlet hair, big expressive eyes and her love shining from them. Bea was small, just a sprite of a little girl, nothing but pure sweetness.

Annie studied her own face—just twelve years old, the image taken when her heart had been whole. Did she remember that girl who could love so easily? She didn't know, she thought, shaking her head. She couldn't find that girl inside her at all anymore. But it was good to be reminded of her. She swiped the tears from her eyes, but they kept coming.

"Your mother was beautiful," Aumaleigh said with a sniffle. "I wish I could have met her. I know I would have loved her."

What a gift it was to have this lady in her life, Annie thought, nodding slowly. As a sob wracked through her, she handed over the locket so her aunt could see better. "I thought this was gone forever. It was the only image I had of my ma and my grandma."

"What a treasure." Aumaleigh studied the inside of the locket, cradling it carefully. "I can see them in you."

More tears burned in Annie's eyes, touched by her aunt's words. Loss was such a hard thing—it took a piece out of you and you were never the same. But seeing her mother's face again, she realized that love never left, it never died, it was not something death could take. Deep in the heart, it lived. It would always live.

"How did Adam get this?" Aumaleigh asked, handing back the locket. "If it wasn't in your things?"

"He saw me sell it." She took one last loving look before closing the locket gently. She shook out the chain and slipped it over her head. Oh, it felt good to wear it again. Adam's letter was still in her hand.

I bought it for you, she read. *I've kept it all this time because I love you. Be happy, Annie.*

Adam

I love you. She stared at his handwriting, at the words she didn't know how to process. Adam loved her? Her gaze stuck on those words and her mind went over them again and again. She couldn't let herself believe it, even as the love she felt for him warmed her heart, spilling over, lifting through her.

"I'm reading over your shoulder," Aumaleigh confessed. "What does it mean that he's had the locket all this time? How long ago did you sell it?"

"About three years." The pain of that day felt distant now. She'd been miserable, handing over that locket to the jeweler who'd felt sorry for her—she'd seen it in his gaze when he'd handed over the five dollars for it. But she hadn't noticed Adam, wherever he had been. Yet he'd been in love with her? She shook her head, not able to quite make sense of it. "How could he have been in love with me then? I didn't even know him."

"Well, sometimes it's love at first sight." Aumaleigh untied her hat thoughtfully, her lovely face turning soft, as if with fond memories. "Some folks sully it by saying it's lust, and perhaps for them it is. But when I saw Gabriel for the first time, my heart just went *wow*. I was never the same after that. I knew I would spend the rest of my life loving him, and in a way I guess I have."

"What happened to him?" Annie asked, curious. She swiped more tears from her eyes.

"That is for a later time." Aumaleigh hung her hat on a peg, turning away as if trying to hide her sadness. "This is about you and Adam."

"There is no me and Adam," she argued, but even as she said the words, she knew they weren't true. Not in her heart. Everything he'd done for her—every single thing. Had he been trying to show her how he felt? *I love you*, he'd written. It was right there in black and white. She stared at it, remembering what he'd said. He'd only been in love once in his life. His words came back to her, ringing in her mind. *By the time I'd got up my nerve, some other guy started courting her. I've only had the one dream and it passed me by. I don't want any other dream.*

Her hands started to tremble, her body began to quake. Disbelief rolled up, and she shook her head against the growing realization. There was no way that he'd been talking about her. She simply could not be his dream. She was nobody's dream. Not the daughter of the town drunk, not the ruined woman who'd believed in Harold's shallow words of love, and not even here, in this new beginning of hers in Montana Territory. Nobody dreamed about truly loving a kitchen maid in a faded brown calico dress.

"You're crying." Aumaleigh leaned in, drawing an arm over Annie's shoulder. "Dear heart, what is the matter? A good, kind and handsome man is in love with you. All this time he's loved you. What on earth is there to cry about?"

"It can't be true." Annie's throat tightened, folding Adam's note because it had gone so blurry she couldn't see it anyway. "How could anyone love me like that?"

"Very easily, trust me." Aumaleigh brushed a lock of hair out of Annie's face, then caught a couple tears on her cheek. Maternal and soothing, she lowered her voice until it was a gentle, loving hug. "That man I told you about, the one I fell in love with at first sight? I didn't feel worthy of him."

"You?" Annie didn't believe that. She sniffed, blinking hard against those pesky tears. "How could someone like you feel unworthy?"

"My sweet, beautiful niece." Aumaleigh hung her head for a moment, swallowing hard, as if wrestling with something terribly painful in her past. "My mother never failed to comment on all the ways I was unworthy. I was young, exactly your age, when I let Gabriel go. Young enough not to know that you are not what others say you are. Other people do not get to decide that. Nor can they diminish you without your permission. You are the one who decides what you are worthy of. And everyone, *everyone,* is worthy of being truly loved. All it requires is truly loving in return."

Annie nodded, touched beyond description by her aunt's words. Her gaze strayed to the window in the door, where sunshine glittered on the diamond-cast snow like a promise, like a whole new and wonderful future just waiting to happen. How many times back in Landville had he tipped his hat when they met on the street? How many times had she simply not noticed him? Regret pounded through her. He deserved more, much more.

And he was leaving. She blinked away the last of her tears. All that time, he'd been in love with her. A man like that, who could love like that was a dream. And he loved her. He really loved her.

"Go to him," Aumaleigh urged, lifting Annie's coat from its wall peg. "Don't make my mistake. Don't let him drive away, not without knowing how you feel."

Adam. What if he was already gone? Desperate panic raced through her and she grabbed her coat, jabbed her arm into one sleeve and sailed through the open door. She hardly felt the arctic cold blasting against her as she ran, struggling to get her other arm into the sleeve. All that mattered was Adam.

There he was, standing beside his vehicle in front of the barn, dropping his rucksack into the back. He was dressed for winter weather, the layers of wool adding bulk to his already impressive form. His Stetson hid his eyes as he turned to her, but she felt the impact of his gaze like a lightning bolt to her heart. He stiffened for a moment, perhaps fearing a painful goodbye but then she was running, her shoes slipping on the icy crispness of the snow, needing him, just needing him.

He swept off his hat, his face a hard, reserved mask. Then his jaw slackened and he was running too. He met her midway across the yard, caught her in his strong arms and swept her off her feet. She buried her face in his strong shoulder and clung to him, the wool of his coat scratchy against her cheek.

"You're wearing the locket," he murmured in her ear, holding her so tight. Oh, so wonderfully tight, like a man who had found his greatest love and was never going to let her go.

And that's me, Annie thought, amazed, incredulous and still disbelieving, but it was true. Undeniably true. Wrapped in his arms like this, she could feel his heart beating with hers in synchrony, as if they were already one. How could anything this wonderful happen to her? She didn't know, but she was never going to let him go.

"I thought I had lost you forever," he confessed, his voice rumbling through her, laden with tenderness and disbelief, as if this was too much for him to believe too. "I was about ready to climb up and drive away. A minute later, I would have been gone. And then I saw you wearing the locket, and I knew."

"You loved me all that time?" She rocked back in his arms, gazing up at him, at his handsome, dear face. "I was your dream?"

"Yes, you are." His gaze turned luminous with the kind of love a woman only wishes for—and it was there, real and honest in his eyes.

A muscle bunched along his steely jaw, making him strong and at the same time vulnerable. "I love you from a place so deep that it will never end. I will love you forever."

"Forever sounds like exactly the right amount of time." Happy, so happy, she pressed her palm against his jaw. The whiskery texture felt so wonderfully manly, and at the contact of her skin to his, a sensation raced through her body, like a sigh, touching her soul. She was right where she was destined to be—in Adam's strong arms. "I would love to have you come courting."

"Good. I've waited a long time to hear those words." He leaned in, and this time she did not stop him.

When his lips covered hers, the world faded away, the winter cold vanished and it was as if they stood in bright sunshine in mid-summer. His kiss was tender and sweet, with a hint of passion, everything a first kiss should be. Love so strong filled her up, it healed every crack, mended every broken piece and where grief lived, it provided solace. True joy filled her soul, and she believed. Oh, she *believed*.

EPILOGUE

Three days later

Aumaleigh took one look at her niece standing in the church's vestibule and words failed her. Verbena shrugged out of her coat, and her sisters rushed in to help her, revealing the pristine white lawn dress, inset with lace. The princess style dress fit Verbena's willowy figure perfectly. The lustrous mother-of-pearl buttons marching down the snug-fitting bodice emphasized her tiny waist. Lacework covered the gentle bell of the skirt and edged the hem and neckline.

"There are no words, sweet girl." Aumaleigh's knees felt weak, just like her over-brimming heart as she held out her arms. Her other nieces stepped back, allowing her full access to the young bride. She wrapped her arms lightly around Verbena, not wanting to muss her long, flowing brown hair or wrinkle the dress. "You look perfect."

"If I do, then it's because of you." Verbena stepped back, a little breathless, radiant with joy. That's just the way a bride should be. Ecstatic, glowing with true love. Verbena gave a little toss of her head. "I never imagined that I would ever wear a wedding dress as beautiful as this. Aumaleigh, I can feel the love you put into it. It's full of dreams."

"And now they are yours." Aumaleigh could feel those dreams too. The girl who'd made them still lived somewhere inside her—time and decades had not changed that. The dreams for true love ever after, for a blissful marriage and babies one day—beloved, precious children. These are the things she still dreamed of, only now it was for her nieces. "Be happy, Verbena. Love your Zane with all your heart."

"I already do." Verbena swiped at her eyes, where joyous tears glistened. Her gaze shot beyond Aumaleigh's right shoulder through the doorway and into the sanctuary where friends and family waited—and the bridegroom. "Oh, there he is. My Zane."

He stood tall and mighty before the altar, darkly and powerfully good-looking in a black suit. His long dark hair was tied back at his nape, his granite face softened when he saw his bride. You could feel the force of his love for her, the kind of love that would never fail, that would always remain true. Aumaleigh's chest ached, remembering when a man had loved her that way. Some chances in life, once lost, were always gone. She'd had her chance and lost it. But Verbena had made the right choice. She was about to get everything a woman could ever dream of—the right man.

"It was amazing of you to lend her the dress." Daisy, sweet Daisy with her molasses hair, heart-shaped face and take charge attitude ambled over and slipped an arm around Aumaleigh's waist. "Does it hurt you to see it worn?"

"No, it heartens me." That was merely the truth. She gave Daisy a little hug back. "Sometimes love wins. There is no better story than that."

Doc Hartwell's fiddle began to play, soft and sweet notes lilting upward to fill the sanctuary. Yes, Aumaleigh thought, ushering the girls down the aisle. There was no better story than true love.

* * *

Annie felt self-conscious in the dress Iris had lent her for the wedding (they were the same size). The lake blue dress was really more of a gown and it made her feel brand new. Not like the old Annie at all. She felt full of hope as she stood at the kitchen door in her cousins' manor and let the cool afternoon air breeze over her.

"It was a beautiful wedding, wasn't it?" a friendly and familiar voice asked. High heeled shoes tapped closer. Penelope, the school teacher, looked poised and lovely in a light green dress. Her brown hair was pinned up elegantly, and her hazel eyes sparkled with kindness. "I came in here for a little quiet too. Whew, that's a big crowd in there."

"It's nice to see everyone so happy for Verbena and Zane." Annie had loved how simple and heartfelt their wedding was. Anyone watching could see how devoted Zane was to Verbena and how incredibly much Verbena adored Zane. The old Annie wouldn't have believed in such things, wouldn't even have wanted to acknowledge it. But Adam had changed that. Adam had changed everything. "What about you? Do you have a beau?"

"Me?" Penelope blushed, waved one slender hand as if to brush away the possibility. "I've been what you would call unlucky in love. I've left all of that behind. Not that I haven't been approached, mind you—"

"By Lawrence Latimer?" Annie asked mischievously.

"Yes, you know it." Penelope rolled her eyes, and laughter twinkled there. "I almost made the mistake of marrying the wrong man, but I wised up in time."

"Smart." Annie detected a hint of sadness there, but hesitated to ask because Penelope didn't look as if she wanted to talk about it. "Who you marry matters more than anything. Especially the kind of man he is down deep."

"Exactly. Which is why I'm happy being on my own and teaching my students." Penelope nodded once to emphasize that truth. "Speaking of which, I just adore Bea. I'm looking forward to spending some extra teaching time with her on Monday. I have it all planned out."

"Thank you. You have no idea what that means." Annie smiled, feeling as if she and Penelope were about to become great friends. "I—"

"Why, hello fair ladies," a man's overly dramatic voice rang out, interrupting. Lawrence Latimer sashayed over, his handlebar mustache so tightly waxed that it shone in the lamplight. A brown suit that was too large for him draped his narrow shoulders, dwarfing him. He bent down in an exaggerated bow. "You both look enchanting. May I request the pleasure of a dance, Miss Annie?"

"Sorry," she told him gently. "I have a beau."

"Oh. Well, I had hoped—" Lawrence shrugged, as if it was a dire loss before turning to Penelope. "My dear beautiful lady, would you do me the honor then?"

"Sorry, but no." Penelope kindly shook her head, scattering the soft wisps of brown hair curling around her face. "I'm not dancing with anyone today."

"Then I will just have to try another time," Lawrence promised, although Annie supposed to any woman in the country it was more like a threat. He bowed again, circled around another man marching down the hallway and disappeared from sight.

"Adam." Her heart filled simply from looking at him. Her soul did too. He towered above her, well-built and muscular, gentlemanly and handsome. So very handsome. His face, sculpted granite, gentled as he gazed upon her. Devotion and love burned there, unmistakable in those dark blue depths.

"I was lonely for you." He shrugged one rock-hard shoulder, his mouth crinkling in the corner as he gave a shy grin. "Plus, I'm a little shy in big crowds."

"Me, too." She held out her hand, her heart strumming. His iron-strong hand wrapped around hers, engulfing it, sending heat scorching up her arm. "I came in here for a little quiet. I hear a good deal of the town's population is in this house. It's certainly large enough for it, but still. That's a lot of people celebrating."

"It's nice so many showed up for your cousin's reception." The tones of his voice rumbled low. "Maybe we'll have as many people come for our wedding party one day."

"Maybe," she said, hope hitching so hard in her chest, it made her eyes smart. "Then again, maybe I'll check out my other options. There are a lot of bachelors in this town, you know."

"Is that right?" The corners of his sculpted mouth hitched up in an amused grin. The steady light in his eyes—the look of true, everlasting love—brightened. He tugged her closer and she stumbled against his chest. His wonderful, magnificent chest where she felt so safe.

"Yes," she teased, laughing. "I already have one interested in me."

"Lawrence, you mean?" Adam's arms came around her, trapping her against him. His grin widened. "I could crush him if he gets in my way."

"Sure, but that would be very messy." She laughed (honestly, Adam hurting anyone? Too funny). She leaned back in his arms, trusting him to hold her. She trusted him with everything—her heart, her life, Bea's protection and the lives of their future babies one day. Adam was the truest kind of man—unfailing, unselfish, strong of heart. She pressed her palms against the sides of his face, feeling the heated texture of his jaw (he was actually fresh shaven for once). She was brimming over with a love so strong, there was no measure and no end.

"Maybe it would be better if I just stayed with you," she teased playfully. "You know, to protect all those other bachelors from being crushed."

"Good idea." He leaned in, capturing her mouth with his. He kissed her sweetly and slowly, so she would know everything that lived in his heart. The teasing humor vanished, leaving tenderness in its place. This was a forever love, he thought as he broke the kiss, a love that would always endure.

"Hmm," Annie murmured, letting her eyes drift open, gazing up at him through her thick lashes. Happiness sparkled through her. She'd never looked more beautiful, radiant from the inside out, shining with a loveliness that mesmerized him—and it always would.

"I would kiss you again," he said wryly, keeping his arms tightly wrapped around her. "But you've used up your kiss quota for the day."

"That's a tragedy." She smiled up at him, with love sparkling in her eyes—endless and true love. "I'm not sure I can make it through the rest of the day without one more kiss."

"I know the feeling." Tenderness rocked him like a tidal wave. There were no more lonely places in his heart. She had filled them up. He didn't know how he'd gotten this lucky, but he would spend the rest of his life being true to her, taking good care of her and making her happy. He'd help her make sure Bea had every opportunity. No one could love Annie more than him, not anyone on the face of this planet. His life was devoted to her. She was his dream, the only one he would ever need.

"Maybe I could raise the kiss limit for the day," he suggested, tugging her in a little closer so that she was pressed fully against him, until there was no distance between them. "How about one more?"

"Just one?" She traced her thumb along the edge of his chin. "I can't convince you to agree to two?"

"Honestly, I was hoping you'd want to go higher than that." He gave a soft bark of laughter. "I love you, Annie. I am going to love you forever."

"Well, I'm going to love you even longer." She went up on tiptoe to press her lips to his. His mouth came down on hers and she clung to him, loving the feeling of being in his arms, against him this close. It was amazing the difference it made when you found the one, the one man who was right for you. The one man who would right any wrongs, devote his heart completely to you and love you beyond belief.

Some dreams really come true, Annie thought, wrapping her arms around his neck. Oh, she was so full of dreams. They rose up like a song in her soul—dreams for their future, their life, their sweet, sweet love.

-The End-

The McPhee Clan continues with *Jingle Bell Hearts*, Rose's story, coming soon.

ABOUT THE AUTHOR

Jillian Hart makes her home in Washington State, where she has lived most of her life. When Jillian is not writing away on her next book, she can be found reading, going to lunch with friends and spending quiet evenings at home with her family.

Made in the USA
San Bernardino, CA
04 January 2014